HARVEY DREW

AND THE
BIN MEN
FROM
OUTER SPACE

HARVEY DREW

AND THE BIN MEN FROM OUTER SPACE

CAS LESTER

HOT
KEY
BOOKS

First published in Great Britain in 2014 by Hot Key Books
Northburgh House, 10 Northburgh Street, London EC1V 0AT

A CIP catalogue record for this book is available from the British Library.

ISBN: 978-1-4714-0223-4

1

This book is typeset in 11pt Sabon using Atomik ePublisher

Printed and bound by Clays Ltd, St Ives Plc

Hot Key Books supports the Forest Stewardship Council (FSC),
the leading international forest certification organisation, and is committed to
printing only on Greenpeace-approved FSC-certified paper.

www.hotkeybooks.com

Hot Key Books is part of the Bonnier Publishing Group
www.bonnierpublishing.com

For Jo

CHAPTER ONE

Space: the great dustbin in the sky.

Galaxy 43b is the busiest part of the known universe. It's also the muckiest. Masses of space traffic whizzes around every day and the crews just chuck all their rubbish out of their ships without a second thought. And I mean *all* their rubbish: broken satellites, dirty rocket fuel, pizza boxes, leftover bits of mouldy food and . . . Actually, I'm not even going to mention what else is floating around out there – I'll leave that to your imagination. It's a disgrace.

Fortunately there's a band of modest and unsung heroes who tackle the globs of intergalactic trash every day. They're brave, they're smelly and they're very grubby. They're the Bin Men of Outer Space. It's a dirty and downright dangerous job.

(Personally, I have absolutely no idea why anyone would want to do it. I wouldn't.)

For a start, their intergalactic garbage spaceship, the *Toxic Spew*, is utterly gross.

It's barely spaceworthy. It's tatty and battered, the rocket boosters are rusty and the supersonic brakes are well dodgy.

The outside is plastered with oily grime that's so thick you could write your name in it. In fact someone *has* written the ship's name in it. Which is a good thing, because some of the huge metal letters that are meant to spell *TOXIC SPEW* on its side fell off ages ago.

Now it says: *O SPEW*.

And you probably would. Especially if you saw the inside – it's unbelievably filthy.

A faint smell of rotting rubbish lingers

everywhere. No, make that a strong smell. Strong as in, stomach-heaving, eye-watering, hold-your-nose-and-try-not-to-gag strong.

Actually, it's probably pointless even bothering to tell you this, because, as this story starts (on Moonsday the 116th of Oort) the *Toxic Spew* was about to be smashed to smithereens.

Chaos on the command bridge

The grotty little spaceship was seconds away from being dragged into the middle of a deadly trash tornado, made up of tons and tons of swirling space junk, and swept away. Like a scab you've picked off your knee in the bath whirling away down the plughole.

It was chaos on the command bridge.

RED ALERT! RED ALERT!

WHOOP! WHOOP! WHOOP!

Alarm bells screamed. But not as loudly as the crew.

'AAAAAARGH!'

Panic on the command bridge

Through the ship's vast vision screens the frantic crew could see the terrifying rubbish tornado looming closer and closer. They wrestled hopelessly with the ship's controls.

'Don't panic! It's just a junk twister,' yelled Chief Rubbish Officer Scrummage fearlessly. 'I've seen far worse. Head for the centre. We'll blast our way out!'

'Are you mad?' cried Gizmo, the Senior Engineering Officer.

'No, just brave!' cried Scrummage boldly. And he posed with his hands on his hips trying to look heroic. 'AHEAD!'

'It's far too risky! REVERSE!' yelled Gizmo. Leaping over to the flight desk he pushed the

pilot out of the way, grabbed the flight joysticks and yanked them backwards.

'NO! AHEAD!' bawled Scrummage, snatching the controls from Gizmo and yanking them forwards.

'Get off my controls!' cried Pilot Officer Maxie, shoving them both away.

'I'm the *senior* officer!' barked Gizmo. 'So I'm in command.'

'Nonsense! I'm much more experienced,' said Scrummage. 'I've flown ships through every kind of space storm in the galaxy.'

'Yes, and all of them either crashed, fell to pieces or blew up!' snorted Gizmo.

'Oh for crying out loud!' yelled Maxie from the flight desk, as the spinning rubbish vortex grew nearer and nearer, drawing the ship towards its horrible fate. 'We're about to be spun to death and whizzed round so quickly that our brains will squish to a mush and trickle down out of our noses!'

Gizmo and Scrummage exchanged startled looks.

'That's gross!' they said, agreeing for once.

Suddenly an enormous plastic tank hurled straight at them from the edge of the garbage whirlpool. Maxie yanked the ship's controls to SHIELDS UP. But sadly, just . . .

CRUNCH! SPLAT!

. . . a second too late.

The huge container burst as it hit the *Toxic Spew*, exploding its sludgy contents all over the ship's front vision screen.

'Flickering spew!' cried Scrummage.

'I can't see!' Maxie switched the giant screen washers to supersonic spray.

It wasn't a great help. Space sludge is surprisingly difficult to shift. The giant washers just smeared it all across the screen, making it impossible to see out. But the crew didn't need to see to know the deadly twister was looming larger and larger.

'You're all going to die!'

'Computer!' yelled Gizmo. 'Help!'

A series of lights on the ship's giant computer flickered on and off, and then it bleeped a couple of times before it spoke. 'Good morning!' it said in a cheerful digital voice. 'Well, it looks like you've got a bit of a problem out there, haven't you? I calculate that's a force 8 garbage twister and I'm really not sure what you expect me to do to help. But I can tell you that on one hand there's a 3% chance of surviving – and on the other there's a 97% chance of total destruction.

'I reckon:

a) You don't have enough forward thrust to break through it, or
b) Enough side thrust to go round it.
c) You might have had enough reverse thrust to miss it . . . But
d) Now it's probably too late.

. . . So I'll wish you a cheery good luck and goodbye. You're all going to die!'

There was silence for a nano-beat as the horrified crew took this in.

'REVERSE!' screamed Scrummage and Gizmo together.

Maxie yanked the joysticks backwards and pulled for all she was worth.

(Blimey, she was lucky they didn't snap off.)

The *Toxic Spew* juddered, its engines screamed, but still it edged nearer and nearer to the deadly twister.

Yup, like I said, any second now the brave little rubbish ship and her crew were about to be pulverised!

CHAPTER TWO

A planet called Earth

A zillion light years away, tucked in a quiet corner of the universe, Harvey Drew flung open his bedroom door and burst in. The draught made a dozen model spaceships hanging from the ceiling zoom around on their strings.

In one awesome move, Harvey dropped his school bag on the floor, front-flipped onto his bed, bounced sideways into the chair by his desk and switched on his computer. It was a skill he had perfected by doing it every day.

Here's something else he did every day: he

checked to see if his computer had picked up any messages from aliens.

(No, honestly, he really did. I'm not joking. I know this might seem a bit mad to you, because you're from Earth – so you probably haven't met any aliens, have you?)

Harvey has an Alien Alert App on his computer that scans the signals coming from outer space. Mostly it just picks up random noises like *shwzz* and *zcherr* and *whhhssshh*.

(Sorry, I'm not sure if I've spelt those properly – but if you have a go at saying them you'll get the idea).

Harvey, like thousands of other people on your tiny little planet, believes that somewhere, far, far away in distant galaxies, there are real live aliens living on other planets.

And he believes that those real live aliens on other planets are trying to contact people who are living on *other* other planets. Such as, say, Earth.

(Oh, good grief, this is complicated.)

So lots of people on Earth are trying to make contact with aliens from the *first* lot of other planets – hang on, or was it the *other* lot of *other* planets?

(Sorry, even I'm confused now.)

SpaceMail!

Anyway, the important thing is that Harvey is convinced that one day there *will* be a message from real live aliens from outer space and he doesn't want to miss it. So as soon as he gets home from school every day he checks to see if there is one.

And today, as usual, there wasn't.

He wasn't really surprised.

Of course the space crew of the *Toxic Spew* wouldn't have been surprised to receive a message from aliens because they whizz around space all the time and they've actually met real live aliens from other worlds.

Interestingly though, they'd never met any humans, or been to Earth. In fact, they'd never even heard of it. But then no one on Earth had ever heard of the *Toxic Spew* either.

Well, not yet . . .

Harvey left the Alien Alert App on and settled down to play Space Quest Android Attack 4. He brushed his curly red hair off his forehead, and his green eyes narrowed and fixed on the screen. He reckoned he'd have time to complete the next level, fly his spacecraft through the meteor storm, battle an entire fleet of evil aliens trying to take over the universe, and save his ship and crew from total destruction before it was time to go to football training.

As it turned out, he didn't.

He was just blowing up the last few battle androids when there was a soft *bleep* and the Alien Alert App icon flashed. Then two words appeared on the screen: INCOMING MESSAGE.

What? thought Harvey sitting bolt upright. And then again: *What?!*

He couldn't believe it. It must be a mistake. But the Alien Alert App icon was definitely flashing. With trembling fingers he clicked on it . . .

And a message appeared on the screen:

From: ∧↑⇨ ∧↺⇧⇷⇺ ✕∪↓↵

To: ↳↔◢↕↔⇨ ↓↔ ◀↑⇨ ⇨↔◀↓△⇨ ↟↔↕▷↔ ⅂↔↓◁⇨△▽⇨↕ ⇨↔⇦ ⇷⇨◢↕↔⇦

(Actually, it was quite a long message and since you probably can't understand it any more than Harvey could, I've only put some of it here.)

Harvey stared at the symbols trying to make out what they meant. No chance.

He scrolled down to the end of the message. But there were no clues there either.

He had absolutely no idea what it said.

What should he do? This must be the first

message anyone on Earth had ever got from aliens. This was a mega important moment for mankind!

It was obviously far too important to ignore it. He had to reply. But what on Earth should he say?

A momentous message from mankind

He wanted to put something brilliant that people would always remember. You know, like when Neil Armstrong took his first steps on the Moon and said: 'That's one small step for man, one giant leap for mankind.'

He thought hard and then he typed:

hello? is there anybody out there?

CHAPTER THREE

Death by garbage twister

Meanwhile, far, far away, in Galaxy 43b, the terrifying junk tornado spun closer and closer to the plucky little *Toxic Spew*. The tiny spaceship was being violently bumped and battered. It shuddered and shook – and so did the crew.

'It's no good,' yelled Maxie, hauling on the supersonic handbrake . . . 'We're going to hit that –'

KADUMPF!

They slammed into a giant piece of yellow rubber. It was the rear bumper of a Mega Nova cargo ship. Well it had been, when it was still attached to a Mega Nova cargo ship. Now it was just huge chunk of rubber.

BOOIIINGGG!

The *Toxic Spew* bounced off the giant rubber bumper like a super-powered pinball, right out of the path of the rubbish whirlpool, and drifted safely off into the inky black of outer space.

The crew couldn't believe their luck. There was silence on the bridge while this amazing fact sunk in.

'Phew!' said Maxie leaning back into her seat. She was filled with a lovely calm feeling – you know, the kind you get when you've just escaped certain, instant and total death. It didn't last long . . .

A disgusting display

'OW! GET OFF!!'

Gizmo had seized Scrummage by the throat.

'We could have died! And it was all your fault!' he screamed, shaking Scrummage so savagely his teeth rattled.

'D-d-d-don't b-b-blame m-m-m-me!' stuttered Scrummage, giving Gizmo a hard shove so that he fell over the captain's chair in the centre of the command bridge.

Fortunately the captain's chair was empty.

*Un*fortunately it had been empty for months because the previous captain of the *Toxic Spew* had abandoned ship. The lingering revolting stench of rubbish had literally overwhelmed him. He almost spewed himself to death.

'You overruled my order to reverse!' yelled Gizmo.

'You can't give orders! You're not the captain!' Scrummage squared up to him despite being shorter and, frankly, a good deal fatter than Gizmo (who was one of those tall, thin, snooty types who look down their noses at you).

Maxie, at the flight desk, stuck her fingers in her ears and started humming to blot out the noise. She'd heard all this before and really didn't want to hear it again . . . and again . . .

'Since we don't have a captain and I'm the *Senior* Engineering Officer, I'm in command,' said Gizmo.

Scrummage clenched his fists and glared up into Gizmo's face. 'Huh! You're just a mechanic!'

'Yeah? Well you're a bin man!'

'I'm the *Chief* Rubbish Officer, thank-you-very-much!' And Scrummage grabbed Gizmo and wrestled him onto the deck.

THWACK, GRAPPLE, GRAPPLE

A polite description of this would be: they battled for command of the ship. Really, it was just a disgusting scene. Partly because of the way they were behaving but mostly because the floor was littered with rubbish. So bits of leftover pizza stuck on their uniforms, sweet wrappers caught in their hair and smears of tomato ketchup smudged their faces as they fought.

Maxie shut her eyes and hummed louder. Honestly, she thought, how much more of this could she take?

'You've got SpaceMail!'

Luckily, they were interrupted by the computer.

'I hate to butt in when you're having so much fun,' it said. 'First, congratulations! You didn't all die! What a surprise! I was sure you were all going to be pulped to a pile of toxic wreckage.

'Anyhow, secondly, and more importantly, you have SpaceMail!'

(It seems unlikely, doesn't it, that the arrival of SpaceMail would be enough to stop an all-out, no-holds-barred, fight-to-the-death wrestling bout. Amazingly, it did.)

The crew of the *Toxic Spew* hardly ever received SpaceMail. They'd sent lots. Well, technically, they'd only sent one. But lots of times.

('Lots' as in several times a day, for weeks and weeks. In fact it was on 'auto send'.)

Their SpaceMail was this:

From: The Toxic Spew
To: Anyone in the entire Known Universe, and Beyond
Subject: Captain Needed
We are on a five-year rubbish mission in Galaxy 43b and we are looking for a new captain to head our lively team around and about in outer space.
Duties: Commanding the ship
Pay: Probably
Skills: None needed. But a weak sense of smell and a strong stomach would be helpful.
Please reply with the following by SpaceMail:

Name:
Interplanetary Postal Address:
Favourite Pizza:

But tragically – no, make that worryingly –
everyone in the entire Known Universe knew
what the *Toxic Spew* was like. And what it
smelt like.

So there had never been a single solitary reply.
Until now.

Confusion on the command bridge

Amazed, Gizmo, Scrummage and Maxie
clustered round the monitor.

From: (this bit was left blank)
To: The *Toxic Spew*
Subject: Captain Needed
Message:
↑⇨↙↙↕⏋ ↓▽ ◀↑⇨△⇨ ⇨↔◢⇦↕⇨◢
↕▶◀ ◀↑⇨△⇨⏋

'Who's it from?' asked Maxie.

'It doesn't say,' replied Gizmo.

'Um, actually . . . what does it say?' asked Scrummage, peering at the line of symbols.

'Computer! Translate please!' ordered Maxie.

The computer whirred and its lights flashed busily for a minute or so while it worked. Then it bleeped smugly. 'What a challenge!' it said. 'But I do like a puzzle. I have checked all the languages in the Known Universe and none of them match. So I've absolutely no idea what it says!'

'Great help!' said Scrummage, with biting sarcasm. They all turned back to the message on the monitor, hoping that if they just looked at it really hard and for a really long time it might suddenly make sense.

Fat chance.

Then the computer butted in again. 'This is your lucky day!' it said. 'You've got a second SpaceMail!'

Another message pinged into the SpaceMail inbox:

From: (still blank)
To: The *Toxic Spew*
Subject: Captain Needed
Message:
↑⇨↙↙⇕↴ ↓▽ ◀↑⇨△⇨ ⇨↔◢⇦⇕⇦◢
⇕▶◀ ◀↑⇨△⇨↴

'Wait a minute!' said Scrummage. 'That's the same message as before.'

And then it pinged in again.

From: (yup – blank again)
To: The *Toxic Spew*
Subject: Captain Needed
Message:
↑⇨↙↙⇕↴ ↓▽ ◀↑⇨△⇨ ⇨↔◢⇦⇕⇦◢
⇕▶◀ ◀↑⇨△⇨↴

'It's someone who wants to be captain!' cried Maxie.

'He's very keen,' said Gizmo. 'Maybe a bit too keen . . .'

'What do you mean?' asked Maxie.

'Well, let's be honest, why would anyone actually *want* to be captain of the *Toxic Spew*?' said Gizmo looking round at the tatty and filthy command bridge.

'You do,' said Scrummage.

Maxie sniggered.

'And you don't?' retorted Gizmo.

'Only because I *don't* want you to be captain! Anyhow, I think we should meet him.'

'I think we should *hire* him,' said Maxie, 'and RIGHT NOW! Before he changes his mind. Computer! Locate message sender and bring him aboard.'

'Really . . . ? Is this a good idea?' said the computer. 'You don't know anything about the sender. There is a high risk he is:

a) a highly toxic alien who would melt all the metal on the ship

b) a horribly venomous alien who would poison the entire crew, or

c) one of those really *pushy* aliens who

wants to kill everyone and take over the ship.'

'Ah . . . then let's *not* meet him,' said Gizmo.

'What, so that you can be captain?' sneered Scrummage.

'Not at all,' said Gizmo. 'I'm only thinking of the good of the ship and its crew.'

'Huh!' snorted Maxie.

'But can I just say that, *if* I was captain, I would say let's *not* meet him.'

'No you can't – because you're not,' snapped Maxie.

It shows how desperate Maxie and Scrummage were to have a captain – any captain other than Gizmo – that they both said:

'Computer, transport immediately!'

'Sure?' said the computer.

'No,' said Gizmo.

'Yes!' said Maxie firmly, while Scrummage slapped his hand across Gizmo's mouth to shut him up.

'100% sure?'

'YES!' shrieked Maxie and Scrummage.

'Mmmmm!' mumbled Gizmo furiously behind Scrummage's hand.

'OK, just checking.'

There was a familiar high whining drone.

(Well, familiar to the crew, at any rate. Not to you of course because you've probably never seen anyone transported zillions of light years across the galaxy and onto a spaceship. You live a very dull life on Earth, don't you?)

The area above the empty captain's chair wobbled and gradually a shape appeared. As the droning noise reached a horribly high pitch, like a dentist's drill, the shape became solid. The noise stopped and instantly the shape plummeted painfully onto the deck.

THUD!

'Ouch!' it said.

'Whoops! Missed!' said the computer.

To be fair, it hadn't transported anyone for months and it's actually quite difficult to transfer someone zillions of light years across the galaxy and land them bang on target in a chair.

Anyhow, the crew regarded the shape with interest. It lay dazed on the deck, groaning and making no attempt to get up. It wasn't inspiring.

'It's not very big.'

'Is that hair or some kind of helmet?'

'What kind of thing has hair like that?'

'It's got funny coloured eyes.'

'And dots . . . look, all over its face.'

'And what sort of uniform is that?'

I know it seems like the crew were horribly rude. But they're from the planet Zeryx Minor and they'd never actually seen an Earth boy before. Let alone one with curly red hair, green eyes and freckles, and wearing school uniform.

CHAPTER FOUR

Aliens!

Harvey lay in a crumpled heap on the floor, trying to pull himself together. He deserved a gold star for effort. I mean, he'd never plummeted onto the deck of a spaceship before, or seen aliens from the planet Zeryx Minor.

(And neither have you, of course. So I should probably explain that although Zeryx Minors look pretty much like humans – you know, they have one head, two arms, two legs, a pair of eyes and one nose [each] – they do have multicoloured hair, bright turquoise eyes and purple skin. And

you don't see many people like that on Earth, do you?)

Maxie brushed two paper cups and a pizza carton off the captain's chair. Then, holding out her hand, she helped Harvey to his feet and onto the seat. Harvey pushed his hair off his forehead and stared around at the scruffy command bridge, and at the colourful aliens.

There was a short, fat and balding older man. What was left of his rainbow-coloured hair was tied back in a scruffy ponytail. His huge belly stretched a pair of filthy green-and-yellow overalls almost to bursting (Scrummage).

There was a younger, taller and much (much) thinner man with short multicoloured hair, a long, thin face with a beaky hooked nose. He was wearing spotless and possibly freshly ironed overalls and a snooty expression (Gizmo).

Finally there was a girl, not much older than Harvey, who wore her straight colourful hair tucked behind her ears and overalls that were at least four sizes too large for her. She'd rolled up the legs and sleeves several times (Pilot Officer Maxie).

Intergalactic GarbleTranslate

Gizmo took control. 'I'm *Senior* Engineering Officer Gizmo,' he said. 'Welcome aboard the *Toxic Spew!*' And he stepped forward to shake Harvey's hand.

But Scrummage pushed in front of him. 'I'm *Chief* Rubbish Officer Scrummage, sir. Welcome aboard, *Captain*,' he said, in an obvious attempt to suck up.

'He's not the captain yet, is he?' hissed Gizmo. 'I mean we're not just going to give him the job, are we?'

'Why not? Anyone's better than you two,' said Maxie.

Gizmo and Scrummage glared at her.

(You haven't been to Galaxy 43b have you? So I bet you're thinking that Harvey and the aliens

are speaking the same language. They're not. That
would be ridiculous.

In outer space they use Intergalactic
GarbleTranslate. Basically, anyone from any
planet can understand anybody else. So in Galaxy
43b there are millions of alien beings from
different worlds who can all understand each
other. Of course, on your tiny little planet there
are millions of human beings from different
countries who can't understand each other at all.

Now, that's *ridiculous.)*

Anyhow, back on the *Toxic Spew*, thanks to
the wonders of Intergalactic GarbleTranslate,
Gizmo wanted to interview Harvey.

'I just think we should ask him a few
questions,' whispered Gizmo. 'To see if he's
right for the job.' And turning to Harvey, who
seemed quite small in the huge black captain's
chair, he looked down his nose and asked:
'Could we start with your name?'

'Harvey.'

'Is that *Captain* Harvey?' asked Scrummage.

'Er . . . just Harvey.'

'But you are a captain?' said Maxie, hopefully.

'Um, well I'm Captain of the Highford All Stars,' replied Harvey, confused.

'See!' said Maxie. 'He's a captain. Let's hire him.'

(Since you're from Earth, you're probably ahead of the crew here. They don't know that 'Highford All Stars' is a football team. And Harvey doesn't know that they think that 'Highford All Stars' is an intergalactic spaceship.

Confused? Not as much as Harvey.)

'You're very young for a captain,' said Gizmo, towering over Harvey. 'How old are you?'

'Eleven.'

'Eleven?!' spluttered Scrummage. 'Multicoloured vomit!' He hitched his grubby overalls up over his huge belly.

Maxie was astonished. She was very young to be a pilot, even in Galaxy 43b, but this boy looked even younger than her – and already a captain! She stared at Harvey with her bright turquoise eyes. 'How long have you been a captain?'

'Two years.'

Counting on his fingers and frowning with the effort, Scrummage did the sums. 'Nine!' he gasped. 'You made captain aged nine?'

The crew were stunned.

Harvey nodded slowly. He was beginning to wonder who these people were and, more importantly, where he was and, much more importantly, how he got here and . . .

'He must be *brilliant*!' said Maxie. She unclipped a digipad from the flight desk. 'We should take him on immediately.' She pressed some buttons and an official-looking form appeared on the screen. 'Here,' she said, thrusting the pad and a stylus at Harvey. 'Sign this!'

'Er . . . why?'

'It's a contract,' she said. 'Making you Captain of the *Toxic Spew*.'

CHAPTER FIVE

The absolute awesomeness
of outer space

'Captain of the, the *Toxic*, er . . . what?' asked Harvey.

There was a short but painful silence while the crew avoided each other's eyes.

'Er . . . it's the . . . er . . . *Toxic Spew*,' mumbled Scrummage, embarrassed by its dreadful reputation – and equally dreadful smell. 'I know it's a little mucky,' he said, hurriedly sweeping some cartons and wrappers off the flight desk with his hand, 'but you can't expect an intergalactic garbage ship to be all neat and tidy, can you? Ha ha!' he added nervously.

'An *Intergalactic* Garbage Ship?' stammered Harvey. 'This is a *spaceship*?' His green eyes widened in astonishment as he looked around the command bridge.

I think you'd be surprised – no, make that 'gobsmacked' – if you saw the command bridge of the *Toxic Spew*.

> *(I've just realised, you've probably only seen spacecraft in the movies, haven't you? So I bet you're imagining a super hi-tech, squeaky-clean ship with stacks of flashy gadgets, run by a brilliant crew with smart uniforms and even smarter brains. Oh, how wrong can you be?)*

The crew looked about the command bridge in dismay.

They saw:

- empty cups and cartons littering the desks
- bits of leftover pizza crust, pepperoni and pineapple chunks scattered across the floor
- broken instrument panels
- grimy surfaces
- the general tatty state of the place.

You know, it's a funny thing, but people can look at exactly the same thing and see it totally differently.

Harvey saw:

- impressive banks of buttons, switches and joysticks
- curious and strange displays on the monitors
- huge vision screens surrounding the bridge on three sides.

And beyond all that . . . beyond his wildest
dreams and fantasies . . .

SPACE!

A million stars flecked the inky blackness.
Mysterious planets hung on the far horizon. A
large misty, yellow one with three golden rings
glowed softly, and a huge, dull-red one hung in
the middle of a shimmering mass of swirling
purple light. The brightest planet was a tiny pink
one which shone fiercely, as if it was furious
about being so small.

Outer space stretched out all around him –
vast and endless and . . .

AWESOME.

He was rudely interrupted by Maxie thrusting
the digipad at him.

'Anyhow, if you'll just sign here, Captain. It's
just for the data records.'

'Me?' said Harvey. 'Er . . . I think you've got the wrong person.'

But the crew thought they'd found the most talented young spaceship commander in the Known Universe and they weren't going to take 'no' for an answer.

Especially not Maxie.

'What?' she snapped, her bright turquoise eyes glittering dangerously. 'Why did you apply for the job if you don't want it?'

'I didn't!'

'Yes, you did,' she pointed to the SpaceMails on the ship's monitor. 'See?'

Harvey looked at the message he'd sent:

To: The *Toxic Spew*

Subject: Captain Needed

Message:

↑⇨↙↙⇕⤵ ↸ ↓▽ ◀↑⇨△⇨

⇨↔◢⇦⇕◢⇦ ⇕▶ ◀ ◀↑⇨△⇨⤵

More confusion on the command bridge

'I didn't send that.'

'Yes you did.'

'But I couldn't have. I don't even understand it. What does it say?'

'How should I know!' snapped Maxie. 'That's your language not mine.'

'No it's not. I thought it was yours!'

'Then whose language is it?' asked Scrummage, utterly confused.

'Computer!' barked Gizmo suspiciously. 'Have you scrambled up this message?'

'Um . . . possibly . . . I might have done . . . just a little bit . . . But it's not my fault!' the computer added snippily, 'If you will keep sending SpaceMails to "Anyone in the entire Known Universe, and Beyond", I can't be expected to get every single one perfect.' And it bleeped off in a huff.

'So,' said Harvey brightly, 'it's all been a big

mistake and . . . I think you'd just better . . . er
. . . send me back . . .'

Maxie considered this for about a
nano-second.

'No,' she said bluntly.

'You can't just keep me here!' cried Harvey.

'Oh yes we can!' She leant back against the
flight desk and crossed her arms. She reminded
Harvey of the girls in his class when they were
in a strop.

'But that's . . . that's kidnapping!'

'So?'

'Pilot Officer Maxie,' snapped Gizmo looking
sternly down his nose at her. 'May I remind
you of the Intergalactic Travel and Transport
Pact rules and regulations regarding replacement
captains?'

Maxie looked at him blankly.

'Basically, you can't force anyone to be a
captain if they don't want to be. The correct
thing to do is to let him go . . . and I'll take
command.' He headed for the captain's chair.

'NO!' cried Scrummage, trying to beat him to it. 'I will.'

'Over my dead body . . .' said Gizmo.

'Fine by me . . .' growled Scrummage. He hurled the full weight of his tubby body at Gizmo and they both crashed onto the deck.

Gizmo and Scrummage slug it out (again)

'Now look what you've done!' said Maxie angrily to Harvey.

THWACK, GRAPPLE, GRAPPLE, THUD!

Scrummage and Gizmo thrashed and rolled around the deck for the second round of their no-holds-barred, fight-to-the-death 'battle for command of the ship'.

Harvey was horrified. 'They're going to kill each other!'

'Yep.'

'Can't you stop them?'

'Nope.' Maxie pressed the ship intercom button. 'Medical Officer Yargal to the bridge, please,' she said. 'And bring some bandages . . . and a stun jab or two.' Then she looked sadly at Harvey and sighed heavily. 'I blame you.'

Suddenly the doors to the bridge slid open and Medical Officer Yargal appeared.

Harvey turned to look at her – gasped, and promptly fainted.

CHAPTER SIX

It takes all sorts to make a universe

'What's the matter with him?' asked the Medical Officer. Her three yellow googly eyes stuck out on stalks from her slimy green body and her six blue tentacles waggled in surprise. She looked like a cross between an octopus and a huge green slug.

'I've absolutely no idea!' said Maxie.

Yargal slithered over to Harvey. She prodded him with a squelchy tentacle.

Harvey stirred.

So she poked him again. 'Are you all right?'

Harvey's eyes flickered open and focused on Yargal.

'AAAAAAARGH!' he screamed.

The crew were stunned and horribly embarrassed. Never, in all their multiple intergalactic missions, had they seen anyone react so badly at the sight of a Yargillian.

In his defence, Harvey had never seen such a revolting alien in all his life – not even in a book.

But it takes all sorts to make a universe, and you really can't go round passing out every time you meet an unusually ugly alien. It's rude. And it's pointless – they're still going to be there when you wake up.

The crew stared down at Harvey crumpled on the deck. No one helped him up. Maxie was the first to speak. 'He fainted! He actually fainted! I don't think I've ever seen a captain *faint* before.'

'He might be the youngest captain in the Known Universe, but he's pathetic,' said Scrummage.

Gizmo smiled smugly. 'Computer: stand by to transport,' he ordered. 'Our visitor is leaving.'

And Maxie didn't contradict him.

Time to go home

'Righty ho!' said the computer brightly. 'I did try to warn you . . .'

'Yes. Thank you,' snapped Maxie. She glared at Harvey. 'Fine captain you turned out to be.'

Harvey scrambled to his feet. Although he was pleased to be going home, for some odd reason he felt disappointed and hurt. Probably because we all want to be wanted – even by a team we didn't want to play for in the first place. And we don't want to be *not* wanted, even by the team we *didn't* want to want us in the first place. Obviously.

'Er . . . sorry,' said Harvey, who couldn't think of anything else to say.

'Yes-bye-thank-you-for-coming,' snapped Maxie. She turned her back on him, pushed up her sleeves and busied herself with the flight controls.

Scrummage and Gizmo went back to their posts.

'Computer: transport,' ordered Gizmo.

'Okey-doke,' it replied and started to bleep importantly.

Harvey stood leaning weakly against the captain's seat and gazing through the smeary vision screen at the awesome wonders of outer space. He clung to the arm of the chair and braced himself, expecting at any second to be flung a zillion light years across the universe and into his bedroom. He wasn't anticipating a soft landing.

Yargal had stayed with Harvey.

'Are you feeling better?' she asked kindly, her yellow eye-stalks waving gently in front of his face.

Harvey gulped and forced himself not to react. 'Yes, thank you,' he said.

'Shall I make you a little snack before you go? How about a sardine and chocolate pizza with barbecue sauce?'

Oh, gross, he thought, but not wanting to upset her he said: 'Thanks, but I'm fine.'

'Computer, why is he still here?' demanded Maxie irritably.

'Because I can't send him back.'

'Why not?'

'I haven't got his address,' it said.

Interplanetary Postal address

'Isn't it on the SpaceMail he sent?'

'No . . .' said the computer crossly, its console lights flickering furiously. 'And since I have an enormous 215 megatronbyte boogleplex memory, don't you think that if it was I might have spotted it?'

'Oh, for goodness sake!' cried Maxie.

'What's your IP address, Harvey?' interrupted Gizmo, looking up from the engineering desk and deliberately not calling him 'Captain'.

Harvey looked at him blankly.

'Your "Interplanetary Postal" address? You

know, it starts with your planet number?'

'Er . . . I don't know.'

There was a stunned silence. In all their multiple intergalactic missions the crew had never met anyone who didn't know where they came from.

(I'd guess that even on Earth that's pretty unusual.)

A horrible thought struck Harvey. Although he had always wanted to be on a real spaceship, he wasn't sure he wanted to be on this horribly grotty one . . .

Or stuck on it *forever*.

CHAPTER SEVEN

How long?

Harvey forced himself to take a deep breath and think clearly. 'Hang on. The computer must have had my . . . IP thingy address, because it found me in the first place . . .'

'Good point!' said Gizmo, and he and the crew looked at Harvey with respect. None of them had ever managed to catch the computer out before.

'Technically that's correct,' said the computer snippily. It bleeped and its lights flickered frantically. 'It's just a question of locating it in my memory bank.' *Bleep. Blibble. Bleep.* 'I'll

have to do a complete search . . .' *Blibble.*
Bleep . . . 'Won't take too long . . .'

'How long?' asked Harvey.

The problem with having a 215 megatronbyte
boogleplex memory is that it can take quite a
while to look in all the nooks and crannies.

'Four years, two months and fifty-seven days,'
replied the computer. 'But that's if you don't
distract me.'

'Four years!' gasped Harvey – who wasn't in
the mood to bother with minor details like a
further two months and fifty-seven days . . .
And he hadn't even noticed there seemed to be
more days in the month than he was used to.

*(Of course, you probably did notice, didn't you? You
might even have picked it up at the beginning when
I told you the date was Moonsday the 116th of Oort.
Galaxy 43b has a very simple calendar system. There
are 360 days in a year. Each year is neatly divided
into three months of 120 days, and the months are
neatly divided into three weeks of forty days. It's a
great system, except you have to wait a long time for*

the weekend. But then Harvey's got to wait four years,
two months and fifty-seven days . . .)

'But what about my family?' he cried.

'Oh, don't worry about them,' said Scrummage. 'They won't miss you at all.'

'I think they might!' Harvey spluttered.

Harvey's mum had cried when he went to football camp for four days – never mind hurtling around the universe for four years without even phoning home.

'No, you don't understand,' said Scrummage. 'We'll be able to send you back to the exact same moment in space and time that you left.'

'You mean you can go back in time?!'

'Splattering upchuck!' cried Scrummage. 'Of course we can. If you travel faster than the speed of light you go backwards in time. Don't they teach you anything where you come from? Good grief!' He rolled his turquoise eyes and hitched up his overalls.

'Actually, where *do* you come from?' asked Yargal.

'Earth,' said Harvey.

'Sorry, never heard of it,' said Yargal.

Harvey looked at the others – but they all shrugged. Neither had they.

Earth: does it exist?

'Computer!' said Harvey. 'Please look up planet Earth.'

'Earth?' asked the computer, and it made a few hurried blips and bleeps and its lights trickled on and off for a bit and then it said:

'Well:

a) I can't find it, so
b) it probably doesn't exist.'

(Can you imagine how worrying it is to find out that your home planet might not exist? Possibly not: after all, you're from Earth too, so you probably don't exist either, do you?)

But Harvey didn't have time to worry about that. Maxie slapped the digipad back in front of him.

'If we're stuck with you on the *Toxic Spew*,' she said, 'you'll have to make yourself useful.'

'Yes,' agreed Gizmo snottily. 'We're not a star cruiser. We don't carry passengers.'

'We're a garbage ship,' added Scrummage.

'Never heard of one. So you probably don't exist either,' snapped Harvey, getting his own back.

The Chief Rubbish Officer turned slowly to Harvey with one multicoloured eyebrow raised on his purple face. 'We are responsible for collecting all the garbage in Galaxy 43b!' he said importantly.

'Yup! We're Bin Men!' said Maxie. Scrummage shot her a filthy look.

'Er . . . Bin Men?' queried Harvey. 'But you're a girl, and they're not . . .' He tailed off because Maxie was glaring at him, her bright turquoise eyes glittering dangerously. He knew that look. It was the one the girls in his class used on any of the boys dumb enough to criticise them.

Maxie raised one white eyebrow and said coolly: 'Well, what would *you* call us then?'

Harvey's brain raced to come up with something that wouldn't offend her.

'Er . . . Rubbish Operatives?'

'Operatives? We're not robots or droids,' spluttered Gizmo.

'And we're not rubbish!' snorted Scrummage.

'*You* are!' laughed Maxie. 'You're a Rubbish Officer!'

Scrummage scowled at her furiously.

Harvey's mind was doing overtime. If he wasn't careful he was going to upset the entire crew.

'Bin . . . er . . .' he stopped. He was just about to suggest 'Bin People' but remembered in the nick of time they weren't exactly people.

'Bin . . . er . . . Aliens?'

'Aliens?' gasped Yargal, waggling her tentacles and deeply insulted.

'OK, how about Bin Beings?'

'Oh, yuck! We're not a bunch of manky

garbage maggots,' cried Maxie. 'Or festering waste-disposal worms . . . or disgustingly gross junk bugs, trash beasties or any other kind of revolting creepy crawlies that might spring to mind. If it's all the same to you, we'll stick with Bin Men.'

Scrummage's rubbish equipment

'Yes,' agreed Scrummage proudly, much to Harvey's surprise. 'We're highly trained, well equipped, professional Bin Men. The *Toxic Spew* might be a bit tatty, but our garbage gadgets are galaxy class. We've got a Nebula 30X-1. Watch this!'

Through the grimy vision screens, Harvey could (just about) see a huge metal web extend outwards and then sweep across the front of the ship.

'That's a mega-strong meteor-proof mesh,' announced Gizmo coming over to join him.

'Looks like a giant net to me,' said Harvey.

Maxie laughed.

'Technically, er . . . yes,' said Gizmo glaring down his nose at Maxie.

Scrummage indicated a set of buttons. 'Now these,' he said, 'operate the Megatron 16XL Magno Beam. It can pull massive chunks of metal towards the ship.'

'So . . . it's a magnet,' said Harvey.

'Again, um . . . technically, yes. But it's very big and, er . . . powerful,' finished Gizmo limply.

'And this . . .' said Scrummage, hitching up his scruffy overalls and grasping a large lever, 'is the Ultrawave 3.2 Vacuum Pump!'

Harvey watched as a giant hose unhooked itself and snaked about wildly in front of the ship.

'We're the only garbage ship in Galaxy 43b to have one,' said Gizmo pompously.

'Yes, but then we're the only garbage ship in Galaxy 43b!' said Maxie, snorting with laughter.

Gizmo ignored her. 'It has three settings,' he boasted. 'Nova nozzle, supernova nozzle and supernova nozzle plus.'

'Wow,' said Harvey, politely.

'Anyhow,' cut in Maxie, 'unless there's something else you can do, like . . . fix the engines, do lifesaving operations in the sick room, actually fly the ship . . . or clean the toilets,' she added pointedly, handing him the digipad.

'Fine,' said Harvey, flicking his hair off his face. 'I'll be captain – but only until you can get me home. And you've got to promise to keep trying.'

'I promise,' said Gizmo.

'Yeah, I bet you do!' muttered Scrummage. Gizmo glared at him.

Harvey signed the contract, quickly reading it as he did so.

'Er, hang on . . . what's this bit about danger money?' he asked.

Scrummage was just about to answer when:

KA-BOOOM!

An explosion rumbled deep in the belly of the *Toxic Spew* and all the lights went out.

CHAPTER EIGHT

Captain Harvey in command (almost)

'Fluttering vomit!' cried Scrummage in the darkness.

RED ALERT! RED ALERT!

. . . screamed the warning alarm.

It was chaos on the command bridge of the *Toxic Spew*. But hey, what's new?

At the engineering desk Gizmo feverishly jabbed buttons as if there was no tomorrow. Which there might not be of course, well, not for the crew anyway. There might not even be an afternoon . . . and the chance of lunch was looking very slim.

WHOOP! WHOOP! WHOOP!

Harvey gripped the arms of the captain's chair and tried to keep a cool head.

'Save us, Captain!' yelled Yargal, flinging herself at him.

Oh, yuck! he thought as green Yargillian goo smeared all over his school uniform. But he didn't push her off – partly because he was too nice, but mostly because he didn't want to touch her with his bare hands.

WHOOP! WHOOP! WHOOP!

'Do something!' yelled Scrummage.

'I am!' bawled Gizmo, pounding at the controls.

'I mean something useful!' snapped Scrummage.

RED ALERT! RED ALERT!

'What's happening?' cried Harvey.
'No idea!' yelled Gizmo.

Good news and bad news

Maxie calmly piloted the ship while alarms screamed all around. 'Why don't you ask the computer?' she shouted at Harvey over the noise. 'You're supposed to be the *captain!*'

Harvey cringed and asked the computer for a status report.

'I'm so glad you asked me!' said the computer cheerfully. 'Well, there's good news and there's bad news . . .'

Everyone froze – this didn't sound good.

'The good news is that:

a) I can get the lights back on, and
b) the ship isn't going to explode before lunch.

But the bad news is that it probably *will* explode before bedtime. And I'm not sure that rubbish in the cargo hold is exactly tickety-boo. In fact,' it added carelessly, 'some of it just exploded.'

'Quick! To the cargo hold!' yelled Scrummage.

'You're not the captain – you can't give orders!' snapped Gizmo, and everyone looked at Harvey.

'Er . . . to the cargo hold!' he yelled.

'Oh, well done! Did you think of that all by yourself?' said Maxie, setting the flight controls to 'auto-astronaut'.

Everyone pelted off the command bridge. Well, except for Yargal, who slithered . . . slowly.

'Wait . . .' she cried. 'Don't leave me . . .'

CHAPTER NINE

Grunge and gunk

The crew ran down a series of gloomy metal corridors, their feet clanking and slightly squelching on the steel floor. The computer had managed to restore the lighting. Not that it made much difference. Half the lamps were broken and the rest were covered with grunge. The dim lighting hid the disgusting mould and grime smearing the floors and walls. But it did nothing to hide the sickly smell of rotting rubbish. Honestly, *nothing* could hide a smell as bad as that.

Harvey lost count of the turnings they took,

and all the corridors looked the same to him – filthy.

The crew were fitter than they looked (although Scrummage reminded Harvey of one of those fat Sunday morning football refs who struggle to keep up with the action).

'Hurry up!' called Maxie over her shoulder as she ran. 'You don't want to get lost on your own ship! How embarrassing would that be?'

Very, thought Harvey.

Finally, at the far end of a corridor, Harvey could see a pair of giant steel doors labelled CARGO HOLD.

Determined not to be last, he put on a final spurt. Harvey was the fastest sprinter on the Highford All Stars team so he had every chance of overtaking the crew.

But unfortunately he hit a large puddle of slippery yellow gunk on the floor, his legs zipped out from under him and he slid the entire length of the corridor on his back. But at least he got to the doors first.

CRUNCH!

'Owwww!' Harvey struggled to his feet and, feeling foolish, snapped at the crew as they gathered outside the cargo hold. 'You need to clean these floors!'

'No, you need to get some non-slip space boots,' retorted Scrummage, eyeing Harvey's school shoes scornfully.

'And what kind of uniform is that anyway?' asked Maxie. 'I mean, is it waterproof, rip-proof, acid-proof, gas-proof – and most importantly, is it maggot-proof?'

'Maggot-proof?' asked Harvey. 'No! It's just my sch—'

'Stinking vomit! You're braver than you look!' spluttered Scrummage. 'I wouldn't go anywhere in outer space without full protective clothing.'

Killer maggots

But then no one would go anywhere in the

Toxic Spew without full protective clothing either. Their green overalls kept them safe from 99% of all germs, bugs and other toxic nasties in the Known Universe – even pink killer maggots from the planet Venomoid Flux.

Which is just as well, because the entire cargo hold of the *Toxic Spew* is one giant rubbish bin. And it's infested with maggots.

> *(I don't know what kind of maggots you get on Earth, but pink killer maggots from Venomoid Flux are no ordinary maggots. They have vicious fangs that rip open your skin and pump pure acid into your flesh. Your insides turn to mush and then they slurp you up like soup.*
>
> *So it's a good job the crew have protective overalls, isn't it? Of course, Harvey doesn't. But then, he doesn't know he needs them, does he? So he's just standing there outside the cargo hold in his school uniform, wondering what all the fuss is about.)*

But just right now, pink killer maggots from the planet Venomoid Flux were the least of the crew's worries. Maggots don't go *KA-BOOM!* and put all the lights out.

Deadly dangerous cargo

The doors to the garbage hold on the *Toxic Spew* are impressive. They're those massive metal sliding ones that look like they've got a gigantic clunky zip down the middle. Above the doors are three orange lights that flash if the cargo is dangerous.

Alarmingly, they were flashing right now, bathing the grubby corridor and the crew in a sickly orange light.

Gizmo turned furiously on Rubbish Officer Scrummage. 'Why didn't you tell us the garbage was dangerous when we loaded it?'

At this point Yargal finally caught up. 'Dangerous?' she cried, her blue tentacles quivering nervously.

Scrummage glanced casually at the flashing orange lights and shrugged. 'I didn't know!

And anyhow it's probably nothing to panic about. Some of it's just got a bit overheated . . . or . . . something.'

'A bit overheated or something? Actually, I think you'll find something just exploded!' yelled Maxie.

For a Rubbish Officer responsible for some extremely hazardous waste, Scrummage could be worryingly hazy on the details. He could also be worryingly reckless. And worryingly . . . er . . . rubbish. He shrugged. 'Don't panic. I've carted all sorts of deadly toxic trash halfway round the universe and back for years and I'm telling you it's fine. We just have to go in and hose it down a bit.'

'We?' choked Gizmo. 'WE?! No way! "*We*" will stay out here. "*You*" will go in and sort it out.'

'Fine,' said Scrummage, and he hitched up his overalls and tried to look heroic. 'If you're all too scared, I'll go on my own.'

Pushing the others out of the way, he slid open a panel in the wall to reveal a store cupboard crammed with equipment – all stuffed in any old how. Out toppled two orange safety helmets, a purple rubber glove, a first aid box and a bright yellow fire extinguisher type thing.

He picked up a safety helmet but Maxie yanked it out of his hands.

'We could all die!'

'Hold it, Scrummage!' she said. 'You've absolutely no idea what's in there, have you?'

Scrummage didn't answer.

Turning to Harvey, she added: 'Captain, if he opens those doors we could all die! We might be ambushed . . . blown to smithereens . . . melted . . . gassed . . . eaten alive or . . . ripped to shreds!'

'Oh, Captain!' cried Yargal, her blue tentacles flailing in terror, 'I'm too young to be ambushed . . . blown to smithereens . . . melted . . . gassed . . . eaten alive or . . . or . . .'

'Ripped to shreds!' prompted Maxie, helpfully.

CHAPTER TEN

Snuffles

'You are the most reckless intergalactic bin man in the universe!' shrieked Gizmo, launching himself at Scrummage.

But Harvey had dealt with a lot of hot tempers on the football pitch. He quickly stepped in and pushed them apart. 'Gentlemen, please! There'll be no fighting on my team . . . er, I mean, crew. Officer Scrummage, is there something dangerous in there? Yes or no? And I'm not asking you – I'm *ordering* you to tell me!'

Scrummage was taken aback by Harvey's tone. 'Um . . . er . . .' he muttered. 'There might be . . . just a bit . . .'

'Oh, good grief!' said Gizmo, rolling his bright turquoise eyes and running his hand through his short multicoloured hair.

Yargal burst into tears, slimy stringy ones that dangled from her face like hot mozzarella off a pizza.

'Get Snuffles!' said Maxie to Scrummage, who went off sheepishly.

(Again – and I don't want to treat you like an idiot – since you're from Earth I should probably explain that Snuffles is a Hazard Hunting Hound from the planet Canine Major. He sniffs out dangerous garbage.

Snuffles is enormous: as big as a pony. He has a huge pink nose like a large, raw meatball and so many razor-sharp teeth he literally can't close his mouth. He's terrifying.

Especially when he's slipped his lead and is hurtling down a corridor towards you, teeth bared, feet scrabbling on the metal floor, drooling saliva and looking like he'll tear you limb-from-limb.)

'Aaaaaaaaargh!' cried Harvey flinging his arms up to protect his head as the huge hound leapt at his face . . .

. . . and then slobbered all over him.

'Don't eat the captain!' laughed Maxie.

'Down, Snuffles!' said Yargal firmly.

'Sorry, Captain,' panted Scrummage, running up and putting the lead back on. 'Snuffles, SIT!'

Much to Harvey's amazement, Snuffles sat.

Warily, he reached out to pat the hound on the head. Snuffles licked him.

'He likes you!' said Yargal.

'Well, he likes the taste of you,' said Maxie darkly.

Harvey ignored her. She was just trying to scare him. He liked dogs. Even ridiculously huge ones with more teeth than the average Great White shark. He scratched the dog under the chin and Snuffles grinned and slobbered happily.

Gobsmacking bravery

'Right, I can't hold Snuffles and deal with the garbage at the same time, so who's coming with me?' said Scrummage.

Harvey didn't think there was much point in him offering since he didn't have a clue what to do. He looked at the crew, one after another.

'Not me,' said Gizmo. 'I'm the Senior Engineering Officer – I don't deal with the garbage. That's a job for bin men.'

Scrummage glared at him.

'I'm sorry,' said Yargal, waggling her tentacles, 'but the safety kit doesn't fit me.'

'I'm the only one who can fly the ship,' said Maxie. 'You're on your own, Scrummage.' And she shoved the safety helmet back at him.

He took it. 'Wimps! You're just scared of the maggots.'

'I'll help,' said Harvey, taking hold of the hound's lead. 'I'm not scared of a few maggots.'

The crew were gobsmacked. Never, in all their multiple intergalactic missions, had anyone volunteered – actually volunteered – to do something dangerous. Come to think of it, never, in all their multiple intergalactic missions, had anyone volunteered – actually volunteered – to do anything at all.

'You're not serious?' said Maxie. 'You're the captain! Why don't you just make Gizmo go?'

Gizmo gasped and gave her a filthy look.

'Because you can't ask someone to do something you won't do yourself,' replied Harvey coolly.

'Vomiting spaceworms! You really are braver than you look!' said Scrummage, regarding Harvey with a great deal of respect. Anyone can *look* brave, but not everyone can *be* brave. Even Scrummage had to admit that.

'Oh, well done, Captain!' said Gizmo, shaking Harvey's hand.

Safety first

'Be careful,' said Yargal, giving him a soggy squeeze. While Scrummage pulled on his safety gear, Maxie rummaged around in the storage unit. She hauled out a screwed-up, crumpled pair of green-and-yellow overalls and handed them to Harvey together with one of the orange safety helmets and a pair of purple gloves.

(You've probably noticed that people from Zeryx Minor like bright colours. They also have no sense of style.)

'Put these on,' said Maxie to Harvey. 'Of course, if the garbage does explode they won't stop you from being blown into thousands of little pieces so small we'll have to scoop you up with a teaspoon. But at least they'll keep the maggots out. Good luck,' she added and gave him a small, quick smile.

'Thank you,' said Harvey, smiling back bravely.

Gizmo punched the security code into the door keypad lock, and the corridor was filled with the horrible screeching, grating sound of rusty metal on metal as the jagged teeth of the giant doors began to judder and scrape open.

Harvey zipped his gloves on, wondering why everyone was so worried about a few maggots . . .

As soon as he stepped into the cargo hold he found out.

SPLATTER, SPLAT, FLICKER, SPLAT!

'OH, YUCK!' gasped Harvey.

'Flickering puke!' cried Scrummage.

It was raining maggots.

Hundreds of tiny, pink poisonous ones plastered them like rice pudding.

'Don't panic, we'll hose off with anti-maggot spray later,' said Scrummage. 'Just don't let them get inside your clothes.'

Curiously, not a single maggot landed on Snuffles. Possibly because they didn't like his fur. But probably because they didn't like his teeth.

Toxic slop!

The cargo hold of the *Toxic Spew* was one huge rubbish bin, but that doesn't even begin to describe it. Quite honestly, unless you've actually been inside a giant wheelie bin – one that hasn't been cleared out for months, if ever – then you're going to struggle to grasp how unbelievably horrible it was.

The walls were stained and streaked with a disgusting assortment of slime and slop. And the floor was so tacky with gungy grime you could actually hear your boots sticking at every step. It was the most disgusting place Harvey had ever been. Frankly, it was the most disgusting place Scrummage had ever been too – and that says a lot.

After a while the maggot downpour stopped, and just the odd one or two plopped on them.

Cautiously they edged forward.

Snuffles seemed to sense the danger and, for a huge and savage-looking beast, walked amazingly carefully on his four massive fluffy paws.

'Steady, Captain,' said Scrummage. 'We don't want to trigger another explosion.'

Scraping pink maggot sludge from his helmet visor, Harvey could see a colossal pile of rotting rubbish in the centre of the floor. Half-buried underneath it lay five or six large metal barrels. They were black, and painted on their sides was a white skull and the words 'TOXIC SLOP'. They looked well dodgy.

One of the drums had obviously exploded, splattering the cargo hold with dollops of a thick grey gloop that was steaming gently.

Scrummage took Snuffles from Harvey.

'SNIFF, Snuffles, SNIFF!' he commanded, and let the enormous hound loose.

Gingerly, Snuffles went over to one of the large black tubs. Harvey crossed his fingers, held his breath and hoped nothing would blow up. Suddenly the huge hound yelped a series of short, sharp barks, and promptly lay down whimpering with his paws over his eyes.

'Oh, that's not good,' muttered Scrummage. 'That's not good at all. I hate to worry you, Captain,' he whispered and looked around, frightened that someone might hear him. 'But I think he may have found some . . .'

Suddenly he froze, and a look of terror shot into his eyes. 'Oh no!' he gasped.

'What?' cried Harvey. 'What is it?'

But Scrummage had grabbed the seat of his overall trousers, and was sprinting to the doors, screaming.

Snuffles bounded after him, with Harvey not far behind.

CHAPTER ELEVEN

Death by killer maggot

They burst through the cargo doors as if their boots were rocket powered.

'Help!' yelled Scrummage. 'HELP! There's a maggot in my underpants!'

Amazingly, the crew swung into action like the well-trained team that they weren't. Maxie grabbed the small yellow fire extinguisher type thing. Yargal rummaged frantically through the first aid box with all her six tentacles. Even Gizmo helped Scrummage strip off his safety gear.

'Hold still!' said Maxie, thrusting the yellow sprayer into his overalls.

'I can't . . .' Scrummage wriggled. 'It'll get me . . .'

WHOOSH!

A fountain of bright green steam spewed everywhere, terrifying Snuffles who yowled and yelped and strained at his lead.

'Aaaargh!' yelled Scrummage.

'WOOF, WOOF, HOOOOOOOWL!'

Harvey grabbed the hound's lead. 'Down, Snuffles, down!' he yelled, struggling to hold him.

It was chaos on the *Toxic Spew* – but then, what's new?

Suddenly Scrummage froze.

'It's bitten my bum!' he gasped.

Harvey was stunned to see Yargal stab Scrummage in the neck with what looked like a metal pen. But not as stunned as Scrummage, who instantly keeled over and thudded onto the deck, out cold.

Ouch, thought Harvey.

'Get him to the sick room!' ordered Medical Officer Yargal.

'I think I'm dying!'

The sick room of the *Toxic Spew* looked exactly as it sounded. A room where someone had been sick – horribly sick – and was too poorly to clear it up afterwards.

Maxie and Gizmo had gone back to the command bridge. But Harvey was worried about Scrummage. He wasn't sure about taking Snuffles into a medical area but soon saw the room was so filthy it couldn't do any harm. Harvey didn't like to think what had caused the marks on the walls and ceiling, but it looked a lot like dried vomit.

Scrummage lay on a bed and groaned pathetically. Computer cables trailed across him like spaghetti and eventually plugged into a Medi-Monitor on the wall. The screen showed complicated charts and graphs.

Weakly, Scrummage held out his hand to Harvey. 'Captain,' he groaned. 'I think I'm dying!'

Harvey didn't know what to say. He was used to players getting injured on the football pitch but this looked a whole lot worse.

Yargal squelched her slug-like way through bits of bandage, old sticking plasters and clumps of cotton wool littering the floor. Picking up what looked like a wind-up torch in one tentacle she shone the beam over Scrummage.

A single sentence appeared on the Medi-Monitor:

DON'T WORRY – HE'S FINE!

'Well, that's a relief,' said Yargal and then, turning to Harvey, added, 'Captain, shouldn't you be on the bridge? I can bring Scrummage up when he's feeling a bit better.'

'Right,' said Harvey, kicking himself. As the captain he should probably have gone straight to the bridge and left the Medical Officer to look after Scrummage. Maxie would be having a good laugh about that behind his back, he thought.

'Er . . . what shall I do with Snuffles?'

'You could send him to his basket but he hates being on his own. Why not take him with you?' said Yargal, unplugging the Medi-Monitor. 'It's up to you. You're Captain!'

(Can I just make this clear – Harvey absolutely wasn't scared of Snuffles. But he didn't know if the hound would do as he was told. Fine captain he'd look if he couldn't even order the ship's dog around, he thought. Especially in front of Maxie.)

So he said: 'Snuffles, to your basket!' The hazard hound nudged Harvey's hand with his meatball nose, whined and looked up with pleading eyes.

'TO YOUR BASKET!' commanded Harvey again, firmly. To his surprise, Snuffles obediently shot off.

(Did I say surprise? More of a shock, really.)

Snuffles yanked him right off his feet, out of the sick room and along the corridor.

'You might want to take his lead off first . . .' called Yargal helpfully.

'Wooooah!' yelled Harvey . . . then, 'STOP!' . . . then, 'HELP!' . . . And then, when no help came: 'SIT!'

Snuffles instantly sat and grinned at Harvey, showing all his terrifying teeth.

'Good dog,' said Harvey, patting him on the head. Snuffles did the nudge with the meatball nose and the pleading look again. Harvey sighed, and took Snuffles with him to the bridge.

CHAPTER TWELVE

Waiting to be blasted to smithereens

'A hazard hound on the command bridge?' challenged Maxie, pushing her rolled sleeves up as she sat at the flight controls.

'Yes,' said Harvey.

Snuffles promptly started snaffling up all the leftover bits of pizza off the deck and licking bits of dried food from the empty cartons.

'Oh, good idea, Captain!' said Gizmo, and threw Snuffles a pizza crust from under the engineering desk.

Maxie rolled her bright turquoise eyes.

Harvey sat himself in the captain's chair in

what he hoped was a firm and commanding manner.

'How's Scrummage?' asked Maxie.

'Who cares!' snorted Gizmo. 'Did you find anything dangerous in the garbage hold?'

'Um . . . yes,' said Harvey.

'I knew it!' spluttered Gizmo. 'What?'

'I don't know. Scrummage was about to tell me when the maggot bit him on the bum.'

'So what are we going to do, *Captain?*' demanded Maxie.

'Nothing yet,' said Harvey.

'Nothing?'

'If I was captain . . .' started Gizmo.

'Which you're not!' interrupted Maxie.

Gizmo carried on. 'If I was captain, I'd make Scrummage empty the cargo hold all by himself, and then put him on toilet cleaning duty – forever.'

'Thank you, I'll bear that in mind. But right now, there's nothing we can do until we know what we're dealing with,' said Harvey sensibly. 'So unless either of you would like to take a look . . .'

(It probably won't surprise you to know neither of them volunteered.)

Maxie drummed her fingers on the desk. 'Oh, great! Let's just sit here twiddling our thumbs, waiting to be blasted to smithereens and splattered across the entire length and width of the galaxy by some unidentified but highly explosive rubbish! Fine captain you turned out to be.'

Lunch!

Harvey didn't know what to say. So he said nothing. Always a good tactic. Scrummage was still groggy when Yargal brought him to the bridge a little later. She carried a stack of boxes in her tentacles. 'Lunch!' she announced. Everyone grabbed one greedily.

She handed a box to Harvey. 'I did you my Supersonic Special.'

He opened it eagerly. He was starving. Which was a shame, because inside was the most revolting pizza he had ever seen.

'Tuna and raspberry trifle with mashed sprouts and curry sauce!' said Yargal proudly.

'Er . . . yummy,' he lied, and then realised with horror that he was actually going to have to eat it.

'Well, Scrummage?' said Maxie, with her mouth full of pizza.

Scrummage coughed nervously, spraying out several bits of chewed pizza crust. 'Um . . . I think it might just be possible . . . that we may have picked up a small amount of . . . um . . . Explo-Foam,' he finished weakly.

Gizmo and Maxie leapt out of their seats, their pizzas flying to the deck where Snuffles snaffled them in a flash.

'WHAT!?'

(I hate to interrupt the flow of the story, but I don't think you get Explo-Foam on Earth, do you? It's cheap rocket fuel. You pour it into the engine, heat it until it explodes and literally blasts the spacecraft violently into orbit.

Well, that's the idea. But usually the ship blows
up instead. So it's banned and no one's allowed
to have any. Not even a teeny tiny teaspoonful.
Let alone several large tubs. If the Intergalactic
Traffic Police catch you with it you're in dead
trouble. Of course, you'll probably be dead long
before then anyway . . .

And if Gizmo had his way, Scrummage would
be dead any second now . . .

Actually, if you don't like violence, you might
want to skip the next bit.)

'You raving lunatic!' said Gizmo, grabbing
Scrummage by the throat.

'Let him go!' said Harvey.

THROTTLE, SHAKE, THROTTLE

GLURCH, CHOKE, CHOKE

Scrummage turned a brighter purple than
usual.

'Gizmo, stop!' Harvey tried to drag Gizmo

off before he actually murdered Scrummage.

Gizmo ignored him.

SHAKE, THROTTLE, SHAKE

GASP, SPLUTTER, CHOKE

Now Scrummage was turning a dangerously dark purple.

Maxie calmly helped herself to a slice of Scrummage's pizza, since Snuffles had wolfed hers.

'GIZMO, DROP!' ordered Harvey, in the same tone that had worked on Snuffles. Gizmo let go.

The crew exchanged impressed looks. Their new captain was tougher than he looked.

'But what are we going to do, Captain?' wailed Yargal.

Three pairs of turquoise eyes, plus three yellow ones on stalks, stared at Harvey.

He had absolutely no idea. But he didn't want them to know that. He was terrified. But he didn't want them to know that either. He'd only been the captain of a football team. But right now, he didn't want them to know that *either*. You have to pick your moment to drop a bombshell like that.

So he did what any footballer does when someone passes you a duff ball: he kicked it back . . . and asked the crew for some ideas.

'Don't ask me,' said Gizmo bitterly. 'I'm not the captain.'

'I am asking you,' said Harvey calmly. 'I'm asking everyone.'

So, while the crew of the *Toxic Spew* racked their brains, the plucky little garbage ship drifted silently through the inky blackness of deep space with her deadly cargo sitting in her belly like a dodgy school dinner.

Some dreadful suggestions

Finally, they came up with some ideas.

'Let's dump it,' said Maxie.

'Pilot Officer Maxie!' spluttered Gizmo. 'May

I remind you of the Intergalactic Travel and Transport Pact rules and regulations regarding dumping dangerous rubbish?'

'Huh?'

'It's forbidden!' said Gizmo. 'We could get into terrible trouble!'

'Not if we don't get caught,' she muttered.

'But what if it blows up a starliner express cruiser with hundreds of passengers?' cried Yargal.

'Do we care?' asked Scrummage.

'Yes! We do!' said Harvey, deeply shocked.

'Could we transport it somewhere?' asked Yargal.

'Where?'

'Who cares?' said Scrummage.

'Me!' said Harvey.

'We'll just have to take it to the Toxic Garbage Dump in the Dork Quadrant,' said Gizmo. 'We've no choice.'

'But that'll take days,' cried Maxie. 'I'm not spending days and days with a time bomb ticking away in the hold, which could splatter us into enough mincemeat to make the biggest burger in the galaxy!'

'I know! Sell it!' cried Scrummage. He whispered to Harvey. 'It's against the law but it's worth a fortune.'

At this point Gizmo had a fit and swore at Scrummage: '!?**! **! ?***!'

(And no, I'm not going to put what he really said. It's far too rude.)

And Scrummage swore back: '!**?*! *? ?**!!*!'

(And no, I'm not going to put what he said either – it's even ruder.)

'Quiet, gentlemen!' ordered Harvey.

In the surprised silence that followed, Maxie fixed her brilliant turquoise eyes on Harvey. 'So, Captain?' she said. 'Again, what are we going to do?'

CHAPTER THIRTEEN

Hmm, tricky

Harvey sighed. Every suggestion put someone or other in danger. He didn't mind for himself – but putting others in jeopardy was different.

'Computer,' he asked. 'What's the least risky thing to do?'

The computer bleeped in an important way for a second or so then it said, 'That's a tricky question. But, if you add up the risks of:

a) getting caught, and
b) getting blown up, and
c) blowing other people up . . .

'Then you get . . . um, quite a big problem . . . Anyhow, I reckon it's probably best to take it to the Toxic Garbage Dump. If you use the B16 HyperspaceWay you *might* just get there before the cargo explodes and kills everyone on board.'

'Right, that's what we'll do, and at full cosmic speed!' ordered Harvey.

The crew exchanged embarrassed looks and then, reluctantly, Maxie spoke up.

'Er . . . I can't do that I'm afraid, Captain,' she cringed. 'We're . . . um . . . banned from the B16 HyperspaceWay.'

'We got caught speeding,' said Gizmo, glaring at Scrummage.

'Don't look at me – it was Maxie piloting the ship.'

'I was following orders!'

'Not my orders!' snorted Gizmo. 'I told you to slow down.' He pointed at Scrummage. 'But someone belayed my orders.'

'Don't you point your finger at me,' said Scrummage, hauling himself out his seat.

'Officer Scrummage, SIT!' ordered Harvey. 'Let's all just keep calm – and think.'

It was dead quiet, except for the sound of Snuffles slurping. He'd finished slobbering up food scraps and was now licking dried tomato sauce off the arm of the captain's chair. At least, I hope it was tomato sauce. Best not look too closely.

After a second or so Harvey spoke. 'There must be other ways to get to the Toxic Garbage Dump?'

'Yes, but they're much longer,' said Maxie and she showed Harvey a 3D digital star map of Galaxy 43b on her monitor.

(If you're not interested in space travel and navigation you can skip this next bit and pick it up a few lines later.)

Since you've never seen one, you probably can't actually imagine a 3D digital star map. And you definitely can't imagine how difficult it is to read one.

It shows planets, stars, meteor belts,

HyperspaceWays and interstellar service stations . . . and it's criss-crossed with hundreds of coloured lines showing different routes and flight paths. Dotted here and there, Harvey saw little red triangles that looked like pizza slices.

'What are those?'

'Takeaway pizza places,' said Yargal.

Very tricky

Maxie highlighted their options on the map.

'If we go around the Megon Meteor Belt, it would take about thirteen hours.'

'Computer, do we have thirteen hours?' asked Harvey.

'No . . . BOOM! Ha ha!' joked the computer.

'Or we could zigzag around the Proxima Major Molten Magma Pools. That would take about nine hours.'

'KA-BOOM!' joked the computer again.

'Or there's the Greater Galaxy Orbital Route – but that's even longer.'

'KA-KA-KABOOM!' said the computer. 'You will let me know what you decide, won't you? Only I hate goodbyes.'

'How long have we got before the cargo is likely to explode?' said Harvey.

'Relax! You've got at least 6.5 hours!' it said.

'Flickering vomit!' cried Scrummage.

'Well, Captain?' said Maxie. And once again, Harvey felt four faces and nine eyes staring at him. The tension was awful. It was worse than a penalty shoot-out in a cup final.

'If I were captain . . .' started Gizmo.

'You're not, so shut up!' said Maxie. 'At this point, Captain, the only bad choice is a late choice. We're running out of time.'

Very, very tricky

Harvey could feel the seconds ticking away . . . and everyone waiting for him.

'We take the HyperspaceWay,' he said firmly.

'But we'll be in terrible trouble if we're caught!' said Gizmo.

'Then let's not get caught,' said Harvey. 'And anyhow, what's the worst that can happen if we are?'

'Well,' said Maxie, 'if the Intergalactic Traffic Police catch us they'll fine us a vast amount of money, make us sell the *Toxic Spew* to pay the fine, and send us all to Glacia Minus – an icy planet blasted by blizzards and snow tornadoes that's so cold we'd freeze to death thirty seconds before we've even landed.'

'Oh, Captain,' cried Yargal. 'I'm too young to be blasted by blizzards and snow tornadoes and frozen to death thirty seconds before we've even landed!'

So am I, thought Harvey, but he grinned at the crew in a way that he hoped would inspire confidence and said, 'So, like I said, let's not get caught. If we don't break the speed limit or do anything dodgy, we'll be fine.'

'OK, but it's your fault if it all goes wrong.'

warned Maxie. 'Computer, plot a course for the B16 HyperspaceWay.'

Full speed ahead

The computer made a few bleeping noises and a very hard sum appeared on the monitor. It was just showing off. Harvey decided to ignore it. 'Ahead, full cosmic speed,' he said.

Maxie shoved the flight joystick forward. Harvey was instantly hurled backwards as the *Toxic Spew* zoomed off. He thwacked his head against the metal headrest of the captain's chair. *Ow! That really hurt*, he thought, but he bit his lip and didn't show it.

Of course, zipping through space at a zillion light years an hour was pretty normal for the crew – even Snuffles.

But to Harvey it was . . .

MINDBLOWING!

(If you don't like technical details, you might want to miss this bit too.

Yet again, since you're from Earth, you've only seen spaceships in films, or on TV. So I guess you're imagining that as the Toxic Spew *went into cosmic speed, the space around it went all wibbly wobbly and then . . . whoooosh . . . it rocketed away into the distance leaving behind a pile of swirling colours.*

Well, that's exactly what happened! Except for the whoooosh. It was more of a zzzzziiiiip.)

Of course, Harvey couldn't actually see it, because he was inside the spaceship. Which was just as well. It's never a good idea to be outside your spaceship when it takes off at cosmic speed. The chance of catching up with it is pretty much exactly zero.

Hurtling through space at cosmic speed was beyond Harvey's wildest dreams . . . It was . . .

AWESOME

and

BRILLIANT

and

**ABSOLUTELY
FANTASTIC!**

He didn't care how tatty the ship was or how scruffy the crew were. He almost didn't care about the Explo-Foam in the hold. Just at that minute all he could think about was that he was in command of the *Toxic Spew* and it was the greatest feeling in the entire Known Universe, and Beyond.

'Steady as she goes, Pilot Officer Maxie,' he said.

'Aye, Captain,' she replied. 'We are thirty seconds from the B16 HyperspaceWay.'

Through the vast front vision screen, in the far distance, Harvey could see a line of lights in the endless starry sky, a bit like a runway . . . then more lights, but moving so fast they were all blurred. As they got nearer, Harvey saw they belonged to masses of spacecraft zooming along the HyperspaceWay.

He couldn't imagine how Maxie was going to get the *Toxic Spew* onto the HyperspaceWay without crashing into anything.

Funnily enough, she didn't . . .

They had only just zipped onto the HyperspaceWay when –

COLLISION ALERT! COLLISION ALERT!

The warning system screamed hysterically.

'Aaaaaargh!' screamed the crew, even more hysterically.

A massive KT90 double-decker space bus was heading straight at them!

CHAPTER FOURTEEN

Heavy traffic

'LEFT!' yelled Gizmo.

'RIGHT!' screamed Scrummage.

Maxie desperately yanked the controls and, at the very last moment – *whoooosshhhh* – the *Toxic Spew* darted sideways and whizzed past the massive space bus, with only the thickness of a bus ticket between them . . . and only to meet another huge spaceship immediately bchind it! And more behind that one, all bearing down on them at incredible speed!

COLLISION ALERT! COLLISION ALERT!

The crew all screamed again. 'Aaaaarrrgh!'

SWERVE...

WHOOSH!!!

'We're going *up* the *down* space-lane!' cried Maxie.

'Computer!' gasped Harvey, clinging to the arms of the captain's chair in terror. 'What've you done?'

'Oh, whoops! Sorry!' it said cheerfully.

'SORRY!?' cried Scrummage clinging onto the edge of his desk, his turquoise eyes wide with terror.

Gizmo was too busy throwing up into an empty paper cup to speak, and Yargal had flung all six of her tentacles over her three eyes. Even Snuffles crouched and whimpered under the flight desk.

The computer's keyboard lights flickered frantically. 'Oh, chill! I just made a little mistake in my sums,' it said, bleeping busily. 'Oh look – I added seven when I should have taken it away. I didn't do it on purpose!' it bleeped huffily.

COLLISION ALERT! COLLISION ALERT!

'AHEAD! REVERSE!' yelled Gizmo and Scrummage.

'QUIET!' ordered Harvey. 'Maxie doesn't need you two bellowing at her. And turn off that alarm – it's making us nervous!'

'Thanks,' said Maxie without taking her eyes off the vision screen.

DART . . .

ZIIIP . . .

The *Toxic Spew* narrowly missed a Stella-Line Q656 cargo carrier.

Maxie sat hunched forward, her fingers flying over the controls as she swerved like a striker weaving round the defence. Harvey didn't know how to pilot a spaceship, but he knew talent when he saw it. *Blimey* he thought, *how can she be that brilliant at her age?* It was only her outstanding skill as a pilot that was keeping them all from instant death.

SWERVE...

WHOOSH...

They zipped around a pangalactic cruise ship with hundreds of holidaying aliens onboard and on its way to the popular tourist planet Verudia.

'Can't we pull over?' asked Harvey.

'That's illegal!' said Maxie.

'What, and going the wrong way isn't? Let's just stop!'

'No! That's not allowed either. I could lose my pilot's licence.'

Harvey reckoned that was going to be the least of their problems. But suddenly the word

STOP!

. . . in massive red letters flashed onto all three vision screens and a loud bossy voice boomed around the bridge.

'THIS IS THE INTERGALACTIC TRAFFIC POLICE. PULL OVER AND STOP!'

'Oh no!' wailed Yargal.

'Flickering spew!' spluttered Scrummage.

'What are we going to do?' cried Gizmo.

It seemed pretty obvious to Harvey. 'Pull over and stop!'

'NO!' yelled the crew.

'We can't get caught with a cargo hold full of Explo-Foam!' cried Scrummage.

'STOP AND PULL OVER IMMEDIATELY! THAT MEANS: RIGHT NOW!!!' boomed the voice.

SWERVE . . .

WHOOOOOOSH!

They just missed a tiny starport taxi. Harvey hardly dared look. But he forced himself to . . . and immediately wished he hadn't.

ZAPP! ZAPP! ZAPP-ZAPP!

Streaks of angry red rays zipped past the vision screens.

'Shields UP!' barked Gizmo.

'They're shooting at us?!' cried Harvey in disbelief.

'Of course!' said Scrummage. 'The Intergalactic Traffic Police have the most powerful NovaBlaster ray guns in the entire Galaxy. And they're not afraid to use them – in fact, they enjoy it!'

ZAPP! ZAPP-ZAPP! ZAPP!

'Oh, Captain, I'm too young to be zapped by the most powerful NovaBlaster ray guns in the entire galaxy!' wept Yargal, and strings of slimy grey snot spluttered out of her nostrils.

Suddenly . . .

ZIIIIP! FLASH, FLASH, FLASH!

The police craft sliced across in front of them, with millimetres to spare, forcing them to swerve right off the HyperspaceWay. Its blue lights blazed angrily and then its giant red brake lights came on as the mighty craft slowed to a halt in front of them.

'Maxie! LOOK OUT!' cried Harvey.

The engines of the *Toxic Spew* screamed and the booster rockets screeched as Maxie hauled on the supersonic handbrake. The crew plummeted forwards in their seats and Yargal was thrown across the bridge and hurled against the front vision screen with a mighty

SQUELCH!

The rear brake lights of the Intergalactic Traffic Police's ship loomed horribly closer.

Desperately Maxie clung onto the supersonic handbrake with both hands . . . 'Captain, help!' she cried. 'I can't hold it any longer!'

Harvey leapt up, grabbed the flight joysticks and yanked them over to the left for all he was worth.

CHAPTER FIFTEEN

Ooooops!

SKER-DUMPF

The *Toxic Spew* skidded off the left-hand rear rocket booster of the police ship . . . and then scraped all along its left-hand side –

SKER-REECHH

. . . and shattered twenty-four blue hazard warning lights –

SKER-RUNCHH!

Finally, it stopped.

Amazingly, no one was hurt.

Yargal hugged Harvey soggily. 'Captain you saved us!'

'Well done, sir,' said Gizmo.

'Good flying!' said Scrummage.

'Don't thank me,' said Harvey. 'Thank Maxie. She's just spent the last fifteen minutes piloting this ship with death-defying skill. If it wasn't for her, we'd be history.'

But Maxie was sitting with her head buried in her hands.

Harvey went over to her. 'Are you OK?'

She didn't even look up. 'No. We are in soooo much trouble!'

The crew thought about this for a nanobeat and then everyone launched into a quick game of 'I Blame You'.

(In case you don't play this game on Earth: there are no rules – you just have to blame someone else either before they can blame you, or more than they can blame you. Or both.)

Gizmo kicked off. 'Fine captain you turned out to be!' he snorted at Harvey.

'What did I do?'

'You said take the HyperspaceWay!'

'I also said don't do anything dodgy – you know, like go the wrong way . . . or smash into an Intergalactic Traffic Police ship!'

'We're all going to be arrested!' cried Yargal.

'I'll be banned from flying forever and it's your fault!' Maxie bawled at Harvey.

'When they find the Explo-Foam we're all doomed!' wailed Scrummage.

'No, *you* are,' said Gizmo. 'You loaded it onto the ship.'

'Oh yeah? Well, I'll tell them you did!' retorted Scrummage.

It wasn't exactly a fun game but at least everyone could play. Anyhow, they were interrupted by the bossy voice booming out again:

'WE ARE BOARDING YOUR SHIP.'

Maxie grabbed Harvey's arm and whispered, 'Just don't try telling them you come from Earth.'

Harvey wanted to ask why, but the crew were too busy panicking.

'My career is over!' cried Gizmo, pacing the deck. 'I'll never make captain now!'

'We're done for.' Scrummage slumped forwards and sat with his head on the garbage desk.

Yargal chewed her tentacles, and Snuffles whined.

'We may as well just give ourselves up,' said Maxie.

Harvey took command. 'No!' he ordered. 'Never say die! It's not over till the final whistle.'

'Er . . . whistle? What whistle?' asked the crew, totally confused.

The Intergalactic Traffic Police

But before Harvey could explain, a familiar high, whining drone drilled into their ears, and two Intergalactic Traffic Police Officers transported onto the command bridge.

They wore black uniforms, dark glasses and

mean expressions. Both of them wore their short multicoloured hair gelled into sharp spikes.

There's something about the Intergalactic Traffic Police that can scare the pants off you. It's probably the multifunctional ray guns tucked in their belts. These have three settings: 'Lightly Sting', 'Badly Bruise' and 'REALLY, REALLY HURT'.

The officers stood on the command bridge and looked about ominously. One of them was a giant of a man who loomed over all of them – even Gizmo. But it was the shorter one that bothered Harvey. He had a nasty look about him. Very nasty.

Harvey knew the type – the worst sort of bully. You know, one who really *does* have power over you, and likes to use it. Harvey had met a referee like him last season. The Highford All Stars were one-nil down in the semi-final, and then Harvey scored. But the ref said he was offside when he wasn't. And when Harvey appealed, he got the red card. The All Stars lost.

'Remember, we're all in this together,' hissed Harvey. 'We're a team.'

'Which one of you idiots is responsible for flying the wrong way along the HyperspaceWay and smashing into the side of our ship?' growled the smaller, mean-looking officer.

In one swift move, everyone pointed at Harvey and said:

'He is!'

Harvey rolled his eyes. *Thanks a bunch*, he thought.

CHAPTER SIXTEEN

Earth: again, does it exist?

Slowly but menacingly, the Intergalactic Traffic Officer walked over to Harvey sitting in the captain's chair and gave him a hard stare. Without taking his eyes off Harvey, he unclipped a digipad from his belt. He managed to make it a very threatening move.

'Zippit,' he growled.

'I haven't said anything,' said Harvey calmly.

'No, I'm Zippit. Police Officer Zippit to you. Is this your ship then, *sonny*?'

Harvey wasn't going to let this man scare

him. He stood up, flicked his curly red fringe off his face, looked him straight in the eye and answered coolly: 'Yes. I'm Harvey Drew, Captain of the *Toxic Spew*.'

'SNORT! HUR . . . HUR . . . HUR!!'

Both officers exploded with laughter.

'You're the new captain of the *Toxic Spew!* They must be desperate!'

'HUR . . . HUR . . . HUR!'

'Where did they find you?'

Maxie shot Harvey a warning look but he ignored her.

'Earth,' said Harvey and the crew gasped softly.

'Where?!' Police Officer Zippit pushed his face right into Harvey's. Harvey could smell what he'd had for lunch (a garlic and apricot jam pizza followed by a mackerel and caramel doughnut. No wonder Harvey could smell it. Thank goodness he didn't have to taste it too).

'I'm from Earth,' said Harvey trying not to breathe in too deeply. 'It's a small planet in a galaxy called the Milky Way . . .'

'Never heard of it,' Zippit butted in rudely, still eyeballing Harvey.

Harvey stared him out. 'Just because you've never heard of it, doesn't mean it doesn't exist,' he said. And the crew gasped again, but loudly this time.

(I'm sorry to keep mentioning it, but since you're from Earth you probably don't know that getting clever with the Intergalactic Traffic Police, isn't very . . . er . . . clever. Neither did Harvey.)

'Now listen, "Captain". If you're from a planet we've never heard of, then that makes you a new type of alien. And if you're a new type of alien then we might just have to take you away and do a lot of very painful experiments on you to see what sort of new type of alien you are.'

Harvey didn't even flinch – he carried on the staring contest. This wrong-footed Zippit. He wasn't used to people standing up to him. Then a new thought struck him.

'Wait a minute . . . There's no such place as planet Earth . . . you made that up!' His turquoise eyes narrowed suspiciously. 'What's going on? You're up to something aren't you?' He turned to his mountainous mate. 'Officer Org, look up the *Toxic Spew* on the Pangalactic Criminal Records Database, and check for any traffic offences, wilful wrongdoings and downright dodgy dealings.'

A frankly appalling record

Slowly, and with some difficulty, the enormous officer prodded his digipad with his outsized fingers.

It took less than a nano-second to access all the records of the *Toxic Spew*. Which was remarkable really, because it was a very long list.

Traffic Police Officer Org read it out, very slowly. Reading wasn't his best skill.

(If you don't like lists you can just skip on . . . I haven't put the whole list in anyway – it's much too long.)

- Parking in an orbit zone
- Flying without lights
- Flying without brakes
- Not having a space tax disc
- Jumping a red light
- Carrying toxic waste without a licence.

Harvey was gobsmacked. The crew cringed as the list went on . . . and on . . . There were forty-seven fines to be paid.

If you added them all up they were worth more than the *Toxic Spew* itself. But then that's not surprising. A party-sized pizza order would probably be worth almost as much as the *Toxic Spew*, especially if you had it with chips, dips and a drink.

'Which one of you is the Rubbish Officer?' demanded Zippit.

'They're probably all rubbish!' snorted Officer

Org, sniggering childishly at his own joke.

Scrummage was far too nervous to point out he was actually the *Chief* Rubbish Officer. He stood up weakly. 'I am.'

'Well, I think we should have a little look in the garbage hold. Make sure you're not doing anything . . . dodgy.'

Scrummage gulped, and the rest of the crew looked petrified.

But Harvey stepped boldly forward. 'Fine,' he said. 'Follow me.'

'Multicoloured upchuck!' spluttered Scrummage softly.

CHAPTER SEVENTEEN

'Flickering vomit!'

Outside the massive metal doors to the cargo hold the orange warning lights still flashed, making the grimy corridor the kind of sickly colour that can give you a headache.

Traffic Police Officer Org stood grinning stupidly, holding his digipad in his huge hands, and looking forward to adding (yet) another report to the long and dismal record of the *Toxic Spew*.

'Right,' said Police Officer Zippit to Scrummage. 'What's in there, then?'

'Um . . . er . . .' stammered Scrummage helplessly.

But Harvey came to his rescue and said, 'We've got six large tubs of . . .'

Scrummage gasped softly. *Flickering vomit!* he thought. Surely Harvey wasn't going to tell them about the Explo-Foam? But Harvey didn't get a chance to finish his sentence.

Zippit spun round and snapped, 'I asked the *Rubbish* Officer, not you.'

Harvey didn't bat an eyelid. He might not have much experience as a starship captain – but he'd captained the Highford All Stars for two seasons and he knew the rules.

'*I'm* the captain,' he said. 'And you talk to *me* – not to my crew. Leave this to me, Scrummage. And that's an order!'

(I'm not sure which of the four people standing in the dirty, dimly-lit corridor was the most amazed. It could have been the two Intergalactic Traffic Police Officers and it might have been Scrummage. But I reckon it was Harvey).

He honestly had no idea he could be that brave. But, knowing that he was dominating the game, and with everything to play for, he kept up the pace.

Cosmic muck and maggots

'Behind those doors,' he said, 'we've got . . .' and he counted the imaginary list off on his fingers as he spoke:

'Six large tubs of toilet waste from a starline cruiser. Unfortunately a couple of them are leaking . . . You might want to watch your step.'

'Oh, yuck!' said Org.

'A large vat of unidentified steaming yellow space muck. We're not sure what it is, but it smells so bad it might make you actually vomit your guts up.'

At this, Police Officer Zippit went a very pale purple and Org looked distinctly queasy.

'And twenty-five bottles of toxic cosmic gas,' said Harvey. 'It's deadly! Just one whiff will

melt your nose clean off your face. I'd try not to breathe in. Anyhow, could be worse. Sometimes we get some *really* dangerous garbage in there, don't we, Scrummage!'

'Er . . . yes, sir,' said Scrummage weakly, and tried not to even think about the Explo-Foam in case he gave anything away.

Harvey punched buttons randomly on the cargo hold keypad lock in a way that looked like he knew what he was doing.

'By the way,' he said coolly, 'are those uniforms maggot-proof?'

The two officers exchanged worried looks.

'No, er . . . why?'

Harvey grasped the huge door handles as if he was about to haul them open.

'Only we've got a bit of a problem with maggots,' he said. 'But I can't imagine you two brave officers would be scared by a few tiny little, deadly poisonous, pink killer maggots from Venomoid Flux.'

'Deadly poisonous, pink killer maggots from Venomoid Flux?' they cried.

'Don't worry,' said Harvey, picking up the yellow fire extinguisher type thing Maxie had used on Scrummage. 'We'll be right here with the anti-maggot spray. Of course, it won't save you if you do get bitten, pumped full of acid and slurped up like soup. But you might die a bit happier knowing that the maggot that killed you isn't going to get away with it.'

He handed the yellow sprayer to Scrummage. 'Stand by, Scrummage.'

'Yes, sir!' By now, Scrummage was completely dazzled by Harvey. In all his multiple intergalactic missions he'd never, ever met anyone as bold and fearless. If Harvey had told him to shove a slice of pizza down his trousers, howl like a Hazard Hunting Hound and clean the entire cargo hold with a toothbrush he would have done it. Even if he had to use his own toothbrush.

Intergalactic Traffic Police Officers are not known for their bravery. And neither are bullies.

'Do we have to go in?' whispered Officer Org

to his mate. Zippit didn't answer. He was thinking, and couldn't do two things at the same time.

Harvey took his hand off the door handles. 'But what about your report?' he said, pointing at the digipad.

The police officers looked as panic-stricken as a bad goalkeeper facing a penalty shoot out. They were no match for Harvey.

'Well,' he said, 'you can either put:

a) You didn't go into the cargo hold because you were scared of the maggots, or

b) You did go into the cargo hold and everything was OK. Nothing dodgy to report.'

And he smiled his most innocent smile.

The officers considered their options and then Zippit said, 'Option b.' And then, because he didn't want to look like a wimp, he added darkly: 'We'll let you go *for now*, but we haven't finished with the *Toxic Spew*, so watch it, *Captain*.'

And they transported back to the police ship.

You know what it's like when you've just seen someone do something incredibly brilliant (or incredibly bad) and you can't wait to be the one to tell everyone about it?

Well then you'll get why Scrummage burst onto the command bridge dying to give the others a full match report.

The crew were hugely impressed but Harvey shrugged it off.

'I just don't like bullies,' he said, casually taking up his post in the captain's seat.

'Oh, and Scrummage.'

'Yes, sir?'

'Get rid of those maggots!'

'Yes, sir!' cried Scrummage and he actually saluted.

'I hate to spoil your trophy moment, Captain,'

said Maxie cuttingly, 'but we still have six barrels of Explo-Foam to get rid of. And we don't have much time.'

'Computer, give me an update on the cargo,' ordered Harvey.

'Of course, Captain! But can I just say, well done! I honestly thought you'd all be dead by now! But let's not get too cocky,' it said. 'Because, right now, there's a 96% chance of the cargo exploding and blasting the ship into approximately 26,000 teeny tiny, little itty bitty pieces . . . in around, oh, forty-nine minutes or so.'

'Forty-nine minutes!' gasped Maxie.

'Oh, Captain!' cried Yargal, flinging herself hysterically at Harvey. 'I'm too young to be blasted into twenty-six thousand tiny little itty bitty pieces in around forty-nine minutes or so!'

CHAPTER EIGHTEEN

Forty-nine minutes or so

'Fluttering chunder!' cried Scrummage.

'You said we had six and a half hours!' cried Gizmo.

'Yes, but that was before you:

a) zigzagged the wrong way up the B16 HyperspaceWay,

b) got zapped by the most powerful NovaBlaster ray guns in the entire universe, and

c) zoomed into the back of an Intergalactic traffic police ship.

All of which shook up the Explo-Foam like ketchup in a bottle! So now you have forty-nine . . . no, wait . . . make that forty-eight minutes!'

There was a horrible silence on the bridge of the *Toxic Spew*.

Harvey forced his head to work clearly.

'How far are we from the Toxic Garbage Dump?'

Maxie quickly called up the 3D star map. 'If we don't have any hold-ups we can get there in around forty minutes.'

'Right, let's go!' said Harvey. 'And, computer, use a calculator to plot the route and *check your sums!*'

I'm not sure that I can convey the mood of utter terror on the command bridge of the *Toxic Spew* as the minutes ticked by . . .

It was the longest forty minutes Harvey had ever experienced.

Maxie focused on flying the ship as steadily as possible and Harvey ordered Scrummage to calmly check the state of the Explo-Foam every minute (instead of frenziedly checking it every two seconds).

Yargal made everyone more nervous by rushing around collecting piles of emergency medical equipment, while the computer asked if anyone wanted to record any 'famous last words' before they died.

Eight minutes, give or take

At last they could see, through the grimy front vision screen, the distant lights of some sort of space station up ahead.

'That's it!' cried Scrummage.

'Computer, update report,' ordered Harvey.

'Well, the galley fridge could do with a bit of a clean . . .' it started in a jolly tone.

'Not funny! How long have we got?'

'About eight minutes, give or take . . . probably . . .' said the computer, bleeping off in a sulk.

'Eight minutes!' cried Yargal.

Scrummage rapidly pressed buttons on his control desk. 'We have to get permission to offload the cargo, and get a dumping bay number.'

Seconds later a polite digital voice said: 'Hello, and thank you for visiting the Toxic Garbage Dump in the Dork Quadrant. What is the purpose of your visit?'

'We-want-to-dump-a-load-of-garbage-including-six-tubs-of-Explo-Foam,' garbled Scrummage.

There was a beat of silence and then the digital voice said, 'Pardon?'

'Flickering spew! We're doomed!'

'Steady, Officer Scrummage,' said Harvey.

Everyone was only too aware of the time ticking away – especially since the computer kept reminding them.

'I hate to worry you, but you're down to six minutes . . .' it said.

Six minutes

'Thank you,' said Harvey. 'But we don't need a countdown.'

Scrummage repeated slowly and with great self-control: 'We . . . want . . . to . . . dump . . . a . . . load . . . of . . . garbage . . . including . . . six . . . tubs . . . of . . . Explo-Foam.'

'If you already have a toxic cargo dumping licence please press 1 on your keypad now,' said the voice. 'If not, please press 2.'

Scrummage pressed 2.

'There is a fifteen-minute delay in issuing toxic cargo dumping licences. Please try later.'

'For crying out loud!' spluttered Scrummage, and he started repeatedly banging his forehead on the garbage control desk in despair.

THUD, THUD, THUD

'Fifteen minutes? We're all going to die!' wailed Yargal, doing the frantic thing with her tentacles.

'What are we going to do?' cried Maxie, and everyone looked at Harvey.

'Try again, Scrummage,' said Harvey, fighting to stay calm. 'And this time press 1.'

'But that's fibbing!' gasped Yargal.

'No, it's tactics,' said Harvey. 'If we live, we'll get a licence. If we don't – we won't need one.'

Scrummage did the whole thing all over again, but this time he pressed 1.

'Please proceed to Bay 14 and dispose of your waste,' said the digital voice. 'Thank you for using the Toxic Garbage Dump in the Dork Quadrant and have a nice day.'

Fortunately the Toxic Garbage Dump in the Dork Quadrant is quite small so it didn't take long to find the right docking bay.

Maxie rapidly reversed the *Toxic Spew* into Bay 14. Literally.

SCRUNNCH!

There was a sudden jolt as the rear rocket booster whacked into the side of the dumping bay.

Everyone gasped, except Harvey. 'Steady as she goes, Maxie.'

'Whoops! Careful!' joked the computer. 'You don't want to blow it at the last minute – ha ha ha!'

'Again, not funny,' said Harvey.

'Oh, cheer up! You might only have about three minutes to live – don't waste them being grumpy!' it said, with a gobsmacking lack of tact.

Three minutes

'Stop counting down!' yelled Harvey.

Maxie steadied the ship and Scrummage switched the Garbage controls to 'unload cargo' mode. Harvey felt the *Toxic Spew* judder as the enormous hatch to the cargo hold slowly peeled open.

'Just a couple of minutes left . . .' started the computer. 'You won't go without saying goodbye, will you?'

'Computer! Shut up!' snapped Harvey.

Two minutes

Gizmo switched the main monitor to cargo cam and everyone held their breath as they watched the image of the huge rubbish removal jib arm shovelling the garbage slowly towards the open hatch.

It seemed to take forever.

It was deadly quiet on the bridge. It was also deadly dangerous. But finally the pile of trash reached the opening and toppled down the drop shaft and safely away from the *Toxic Spew*. Everyone leapt up and cheered with relief.

They'd done it!

KA-BOOM!

Or maybe they hadn't . . .

CHAPTER NINETEEN

Out of control

RED ALERT! RED ALERT!

WHOOP! WHOOP! WHOOP!

The ship was whizzing round wildly like a balloon that's been blown up and then let go (except it didn't make that rude farting noise balloons make). And worse, they were rocketing through space – completely out of control! Maxie wrestled with the flight controls. 'I can't stop it!' she cried.

Everyone clung on for dear life as they spun

round faster and faster. Harvey shut his eyes. His stomach was struggling to keep up with the rest of him.

'I'm going to vomit!' announced Gizmo.

'Mulitcoloured upchuck!' cried Scrummage.

'Yes, probably!' agreed Medical Officer Yargal.

(Guess what – it was chaos on the command bridge of the *Toxic Spew*. But hey, what's new?)

Harvey forced himself to open his eyes and look through the vision screen at the stars and planets spinning round crazily. He immediately wished he hadn't. He also wished he hadn't eaten Yargal's Supersonic Special. A hot rush of sickness swept over him and the pizza threatened to reappear. It had been bad enough seeing it the first time.

It's a good job the *Toxic Spew* has a powerful artificial gravity system. Otherwise the crew would have been flung to the sides of the command bridge and whizzed round like clothes in a washing machine set to 'super spin'.

DAMAGE ALERT! DAMAGE ALERT!

. . . shrieked the warning system.

'Computer! Cut the alarms and give me a status report!' ordered Harvey.

'Oh dear,' it said. 'It's all gone *horribly* wrong. On the one hand you were lucky the Explo-Foam didn't blow up *inside* the cargo hold. But on the other hand you were very unlucky that a nanosecond after you had dumped the stuff, it *did* explode – and slap-bang next to the left-hand engine. Which is now either:

   a) shattered
   b) wrecked, or
   c) bust.'

'Can we fix it?' asked Harvey.

'How would I know? I'm not the Senior Engineering Officer!' snapped the computer and bleeped off.

'Captain, I'm not sure I can repair it,' said

Gizmo through clenched teeth, trying not to throw up. 'But the other engine is still working.'

'Which is why we're whizzing round so fast our guts are going to tangle into a knot of knitting and we'll be strangled to death by our own innards!' yelled Maxie, still battling at the flight desk.

'If we carry on spinning we'll damage the other engine too!' warned Gizmo.

'In that case, cut power to both engines!' demanded Harvey.

Gizmo did, and the *Toxic Spew* slowly stopped spinning, and began drifting aimlessly through the darkness of outer space.

Lost in space

They had no idea where they were. The blast had hurled them, spiralling, a gazillion miles across outer space. The blackness through the vision screen was dotted with strange distant planets and unfamiliar stars. Maxie was using the 3D star map trying to work out where in the universe they had ended up. Fat chance. It's hard enough finding where you are on a 3D star map when you know where you are in the first place.

The trouble with being lost in space is that there aren't any helpful signs saying 'Straight on for the Gallipian Nebula' or 'Planet Pandromeda left at the roundabout'. And it's not like you can open a window and ask a boy on a bike.

While Maxie checked the star map, Gizmo tried to find out why the left-hand engine had stopped. He tried every test in the book (the book was *The Idiot's Guide to Space Engines*). He even tried turning it on and off few times, unplugging it completely and thumping the engineering desk. Nothing worked.

'Captain,' he said grimly. 'It's broken.'

(If you're not mechanically minded you could miss the next sentence – it won't mean much to you anyway.)

'It's either the hyperdrive gearing nodes or the mega-drivebelt or maybe the nova-drive robotic plates,' he said.

Harvey looked over Gizmo's shoulder at the image of the engine on his monitor and tried to understand him. Then he noticed something.

'Um . . . what's that?' He pointed to a dark splodge on the screen.

Scrummage went over and all three of them peered at the shadowy blob.

'That? Oh . . . ah . . .' said Gizmo pretending he'd seen this already. 'Or . . . it could be something stuck in the engine!'

'Looks like a chunk from an Explo-Foam tub to me,' said Scrummage drily.

It was. And you don't need to be a space mechanic – sorry, 'Senior Engineering Officer' – to know that engines don't work very well if they've got clumps of metal stuck in them.

Gizmo groaned. This was his worst nightmare. If there was any damage to the engines it was his job to fix them – even if that meant going outside. 'Outside' as in 'out of the ship and into the vast and terrifying inky-black nothingness of outer space'. It's not that he's a wimp. It's just that when you're flying around the galaxy, nice and safe inside a spaceship, you kind of want to stay inside – where it's . . . well, nice and safe.

(I'm sorry to bring it up again but since you're from Earth, you're probably wondering just how dangerous and scary it is to do repairs on the outside of a spaceship in deep space. The answer is: very.

Think about it. How would you like to clamber out of a plane to fix a broken engine . . . while the plane is actually flying thousands of miles up in the sky . . . and in the dark? I'm guessing not much.)

Going outside

Gizmo had no choice. If he had, you can bet your pet hamster he would have stayed inside. For several moments Gizmo just sat gazing at the image of the broken engine on his monitor, trying to ignore the fact that the rest of the crew were looking at him expectantly.

'What are you waiting for, *Senior* Engineering Officer Gizmo?' sneered Scrummage. 'That engine won't come to you!'

'Gizmo, are you all right?' asked Maxie quietly.

'Yes, fine . . . er, thank you. Right then,' he said limply. 'I'll go and get kitted up and, er . . . go outside then.' Reluctantly he headed for the doorway of the bridge.

Harvey followed him. 'I'll help.'

If you'd slapped the entire crew round their faces, one after another, with a raw quarter-pound beef burger they couldn't have been more surprised. Never in all their multiple intergalactic missions had anyone ever, EVER, volunteered to go outside.

'You don't have to do that, Captain! It's my job,' said Gizmo bravely.

'Yes, it's *his* job!' said Scrummage, meanly.

'I know,' said Harvey. 'But it's my job to

support my team . . . er . . . crew.' He headed off the bridge. 'Let's go, Gizmo.'

'Yes, sir. Thank you, sir!' said Gizmo, who was more grateful (and more gobsmacked) than he'd ever been in his entire life.

CHAPTER TWENTY

Spacewalk!

The exit pod of the *Toxic Spew* looks like a grubby, short, round tunnel. The plasti-glass window in the door is smeared with finger marks and odd splatters of . . . well, frankly, who knows? Harvey peered in. On the far side he could just make out the large circular door hatch. A jumble of grubby space suits, helmets, boots and backpacks cluttered the floor. It looked like the Highford All Stars changing room after a really rough match.

Gizmo slid open the airlock and Harvey

followed him in. Then it *swooooshed* closed behind them.

(Can you imagine how Harvey felt about doing his first spacewalk? He was 'over the moon' [actually, he really was over the moon. Over the moon and about 3.7 gazillion light years away, to the left])

Harvey could hear his heart pounding in his ears. But he forced himself to watch carefully as Gizmo clambered into his silver space suit. Harvey had no idea how to put one on, but he didn't want Gizmo to know that.

The *Toxic Spew* is kitted out with Super Economy Space Suits. They're all the same size: Large (or in Harvey's case: Much Too Large). They have built-in gloves and sealed boots to make them airtight.

It's absolutely *vital* to put the life support pack on properly. Basically, there are two crucial hoses. The oxygen one goes into the helmet, and the other one (for poos and wees) goes . . . er . . . somewhere else.

Whatever you do, you don't want to get these two pipes muddled up.

Once they'd scrambled into their space suits, they clipped on their lifelines.

(Since you're from Earth – and I promise that's the last time I'm going to mention it – I should probably explain that a 'lifeline' is just a posh space word for a long bit of old nylon rope. You tie one end onto your belt and the other onto the ship. Not very technical, I know, but probably the most important piece of an astronaut's kit.)

The absolute nothingness of outer space

Gizmo checked to make sure both lifelines were firmly attached, then he opened the exit hatch and they stepped out of the spaceship into . . . nothing . . . the absolute nothingness that is outer space. Airless and silent and empty – except for a million stars and planets stretching out endlessly, and of course, one tatty little intergalactic garbage ship, which was comfortingly near.

For Harvey it was . . .

MINDBLOWING!

And also embarrassing. Moving about was much harder than he'd expected. He thought it would be like swimming, where you push or pull yourself through the water. But in space there's nothing to push against, so you just float there waving your arms and legs, and looking ridiculous.

Gizmo was confidently pulling himself along the side of the *Toxic Spew* by hanging onto any sticky-out bits. It's a risky tactic. Some of the sticky-out bits were so battered and wobbly they might well have broken off.

Harvey couldn't get the hang of it. His legs caught in his lifeline so he let go of the ship to sort them out, and immediately started somersaulting backwards.

He heard Gizmo's voice through his helmet radio.

'Are you all right, Captain?'

'Yes, fine, thank you,' said Harvey, who was by now completely upside down and hopelessly tangled.

'Only, you seem to be having a bit of trouble,' continued Gizmo. He helped Harvey roll the right way up and then gently shoved him back to the ship.

'It's best to hold on, Captain.'

'Of course,' replied Harvey, grabbing onto some sort of metal thingy on the side of the *Toxic Spew*.

They hauled themselves round to the huge metal case of the left-hand engine. They could easily see the chunk of metal jammed into the side. But they couldn't reach it.

(You would think, wouldn't you, that people who build spaceships would make sure the lifeline cables are long enough to reach all the really useful bits on the outside of the ship? Well, they don't.

On the Toxic Spew *the cables are about two*

metres shorter than the distance from the exit pod to the left-hand engine. Worrying, isn't it? It was for Harvey and Gizmo.)

Stretched to breaking point

Meanwhile, Maxie and the others sat anxiously on the command bridge. They couldn't see Gizmo and Harvey so they didn't have a clue what was happening. Maxie nervously chewed her nails and Yargal sucked noisily on one of her tentacles.

'Do you have to do that?' snapped Scrummage.

'Yes we do!' said Maxie. 'If it bothers you, then perhaps you can go somewhere else. You know, like outside . . . with the others.'

'You should be out there helping Gizmo,' said Yargal. 'Not the Captain. It was your fault.'

'No it wasn't!'

'Don't start,' snapped Maxie, whose nerves were stretched to breaking point. 'I'm going to radio them. Bridge to Gizmo, can you hear me?'

There was no reply.

(Look, I don't want to make a big drama out of this moment – don't worry, nothing bad had happened. It was just that Harvey and Gizmo were too busy having a massive row to hear her.)

'Are you crazy?' cried Gizmo.

'Only for about a minute! Just as long as it takes me to get to that bit of metal and give it a shove.'

'No! It's rule one of the Intergalactic Travel and Transport Pact rules and regulations regarding repairs outside a spaceship. NEVER UNCLIP YOUR LIFELINE.'

'Do you have a better idea?'

'Er . . . no.'

'Well, then,' said Harvey, unclipping his lifeline and handing it to Gizmo. 'Don't worry, I'll be fine.'

Gizmo watched Harvey haul himself towards the engine. 'Just don't let go of the ship, Captain!' he said.

For goodness sake, I'm not that stupid! thought Harvey.

Harvey edged his way round and, clinging onto the side of the engine casing with one hand, jiggled the lump of metal with the other. It was quite loose. It just needed a good hard shove.

So Harvey gave it a good hard shove – with both hands.

Which was a mistake. A big mistake. Actually, it was . . . the biggest mistake of his life.

Because the metal chunk broke away much more easily than he'd expected . . . and Harvey plummeted after it! He made a frantic grab for the ship, but too late, and his fingers closed on . . . nothing!

'Gizmo! Help!'

Gizmo kicked against the ship and launched himself as hard as he could towards Harvey, but he could only go as far as his lifeline would let him. Desperately, they lunged for each other's outstretched hands . . . but missed – by about half a centimetre . . .

. . . and Harvey floated off into space.

'Captain!' cried Gizmo. 'Captain!'

CHAPTER TWENTY-ONE

'I've lost the Captain!'

Maxie kept on trying to get Gizmo on the radio. Scrummage and Yargal waited nervously. And at last they heard his voice. Which should have been a huge relief. But wasn't, because he said:

'I've lost the Captain!'

'What?!' wailed Yargal.

'How?!' spluttered Scrummage.

'He unclipped his lifeline.'

'Why did you let him do that?' cried Maxie.

'Splattering sick buckets! You did it on purpose!' cried Scrummage. 'So that you can be captain!'

'I did not. How dare you!'

Yargal sobbed and flailed her tentacles hysterically. 'Do something, someone!'

'Calm down!' snapped Maxie. 'We have to find him.'

They urgently looked through the vision screens around the command bridge, hoping they could locate Harvey. They couldn't.

'Gizmo, can you still see him?' asked Scrummage.

'He's about fifty metres away from the left-hand engine.'

Maxie switched the flight desk monitor to Space-Scan. There were two slowly moving blips – one was just drifting along and the other was gently turning backward somersaults.

'That's him!' she cried. 'Computer, lock onto the captain, and bring him back onboard!'

'Don't be silly!' snapped the computer. 'I can't transport a person who's revolving round like a Catherine wheel! He'll get all scrambled and end up with his ears on his knees, or his feet on back to front, or his fingers up his nose . . . or even worse.'

'What are we going to do?' cried Yargal.

The crew exchanged horrified looks. But no one had a clue.

Which was a shame, because Harvey's fate was in their hands.

Captain adrift

Harvey watched the *Toxic Spew* drift further and further away.

It was the first time he'd seen it properly from the outside. He hadn't realised how grubby and battered and tatty it was. He could just make out what was left of its name, in massive yellow capital letters:

O SPEW.

Yup, O Spew! he thought. *I couldn't have put it better.*

It can be very peaceful drifting about in space, just kicking back and watching the stars and planets against the pitch-black of a deep space sky. But not if you've lost all contact with your ship and you're suddenly overwhelmed by the dreadful fear that you might never, ever get to go home.

This is it, thought Harvey in despair. *Forever! Mum's never going to cook me bangers and mash again, or double chocolate birthday cake with chocolate icing, chocolate buttons and mini marshmallows. No more birthdays . . . no more football with the Highford All Stars . . . no more Dad cheering at the match . . .*

'NOOOOOOOO!!' he screamed.

But in space, no one can hear you scream.

Unless they've got a radio in their helmet of course.

'OOOOOWWW!' Gizmo's eardrums nearly exploded inside his head.

'Oooops! Sorry!'

'Don't worry, Captain. We'll soon get you back onboard.'

'How?'

'Um . . .' said Gizmo. *I have absolutely no idea*, he thought. But he wasn't going to tell Harvey that. 'Don't you worry about minor details like that,' he said. 'Leave it to us.'

Back on the command bridge, Maxie slowly steered the *Toxic Spew* around so that they could at least see Harvey through the vision screens.

'There he is!' cried Yargal. They watched helplessly as Harvey floated away, gradually getting smaller and smaller . . .

'I know he's the captain, but he seems so tiny and helpless!' sobbed Yargal snotting strings of sticky tears out of her nostrils.

'There must be something we can do!' said Maxie desperately.

'Like what?' said Scrummage.

CHAPTER TWENTY-TWO

Never say die

Back at the exit pod Gizmo was trying hard to make radio contact with Harvey. 'Captain, can you hear me?'

But all he got in reply was: 'Sswcheer-ing bzz Giz-rchhhh!'

'He's out of radio range!' Gizmo told the others on the bridge.

'Computer?' said Maxie. 'Any ideas?'

'Yes! Advertise for another captain!' it said. 'You won't get that one back.'

'NO!' snapped Maxie angrily and she

thumped both her fists on the flight desk. 'We *must* get him back.

'Look, Harvey didn't even want to be our captain,' she went on. 'He came here by mistake and we *promised* that one day we would get him home. He's a brilliant captain, and brave. He's risked his life for us and we're not going to abandon him.'

'Maxie's right!' cried Yargal, suddenly pulling herself together, her three eyes wobbling angrily on their stalks. '"Never say die!" as Captain Harvey would say, and . . . and . . . "It's not over till the final whistle" . . . er . . . whatever that means.

'And we are not going to give up. Gizmo – keep trying the radio. Maxie – get this ship as close to him as you can. And Scrummage – you just think of a way to get him back onboard. And quickly!'

And she gave Scrummage a mighty whack round the back of his head with one of her tentacles.

THWACK!

'Ouch!'

Out cold

Five hundred or so metres out in space, Harvey could just make out the worried faces of Maxie and Yargal through the vision screen. So he waved at them bravely and thought he saw them wave back, Yargal's tentacles flailing wildly.

Scrummage wasn't waving. He was thinking.

'Splattering sickbags!' he said. 'I've got an idea!' He rapidly flicked switches and punched buttons on the garbage control desk.

A small distance away, Harvey watched in utter dismay as the *Toxic Spew* drifted off. It seemed so small that it looked like one of the model spaceships in his bedroom back home.

Then he noticed that he seemed to be getting

nearer the ship – and rather quickly . . . and then worryingly quickly . . . and then terrifyingly quickly!

Luckily he didn't have time to take this in before:

RU-UUU-UUUSH! CLANG!

Harvey's space helmet walloped against the *Toxic Spew*'s massive Megatron 16XL Magno Beam, with enough force to dent the metal, bring tears to his eyes – and knock him out cold.

Totally unaware of what was happening, Harvey dangled from the giant magnet, his space helmet stuck to it like superglue. Slowly the Megatron 16XL swung round to the exit pod and Gizmo grabbed hold of his legs.

'I've got him, Scrummage! Turn off the Magno Beam.' And when Harvey dropped off the giant magnet, Gizmo hauled him safely inside.

On the command bridge the crew burst out cheering.

'Good thinking, Scrummage,' cried Maxie, and much to his surprise she hugged him.

Yargal also tried to give Scrummage one of her slimy hugs, but he was too quick for her and stepped aside. 'Er . . . don't you think you should go and see if the captain's all right?' he asked.

So the Medical Officer slithered off, taking Snuffles with her.

You can't win 'em all

Sometime later, Harvey woke up in the sick room. Yargal loomed over him, dripping green slime (yuck) and gently prodding his face with a slimy tentacle (even more yuck). His head was pounding, and he ached all over. But worse, much worse than this, his legs felt funny, like they were being crushed. What if he couldn't walk? What if he could never play football again?

'Yargal! I can't move my legs!' he cried.

'Get off, Snuffles!' said Yargal and hauled the huge Hazard Hunting Hound off Harvey's legs and onto the floor.

Harvey sighed with relief and sat up.

'How are you feeling?' asked Yargal kindly, putting a large plastic pillow behind his back to prop him up. 'Could you manage to eat something?'

Harvey knew exactly what he wanted. 'Can you do: bangers and mash followed by double chocolate birthday cake with chocolate icing, chocolate buttons and mini marshmallows?'

Yargal did her best and a few minutes later proudly presented Harvey with a large, deep pan, double chocolate and sausage pizza with mashed potato, chocolate buttons and marshmallows on top.

Oh well, thought Harvey. *You can't win 'em all.*

Where to?

It was calm and peaceful on the command bridge of the *Toxic Spew*.

Hey, that *is* new.

Maxie had finally managed to pinpoint their position and the computer was standing by, awaiting captain's orders, to plot a course back towards Galaxy 43b.

Beyond the grimy vision screens, millions of stars and a dozen strange planets shimmered and shone peacefully in the cosmic darkness.

Gizmo double-checked the repairs to the left-hand engine while Scrummage snoozed with his feet up on the garbage control desk. Maxie was beating the computer at a complicated maze game. The computer was sulking.

The doors to the command bridge slid open and Harvey walked in, followed by Yargal and Snuffles.

'Anything to report?' he asked, settling himself into the captain's chair.

Gizmo stood to attention. 'Engines all fired up and raring to go, sir!'

Scrummage woke up with a start and almost fell off his seat. 'Splattering upchuck,' he cried, leaping up. 'Welcome back to the bridge, sir.'

Maxie gave him a grin from the flight desk where she was waiting for his orders. 'So, Captain,' she said. 'Where are we heading?'

Harvey didn't need to give it a second thought. He knew exactly where he wanted to go. So he said: 'Computer, have you managed to find out how to send me home?'

Is this Earth?

The computer bleeped and its console lights flicked on and off importantly. 'I'm glad you asked me that, Captain,' it said smugly. 'Well, there's good news and there's bad news.'

Uh-oh, thought Harvey. *I so don't like the sound of this.*

'The bad news is I haven't *actually* found

your Interplanetary Postal address. But the good news is that I think I've found the tiny little planet you call "Earth".'

'You have? Yes!' cried Harvey, punching the air. Home! He was going home!

The computer continued: 'If we go towards the poisonous gas clouds of Novum 12 . . . and turn left at the Star Clusters of Milinia . . . go over the intergalactic roundabout System 17 . . . Is the planet you call "Earth" the large orange planet with three moons?'

'No,' said Harvey.

'Are you sure?'

'Yes.'

'Oh,' said the computer and bleeped off.

Harvey sighed and slumped back into the captain's chair in utter disappointment. He was gutted.

'Bad luck, Captain,' said Yargal, and she slid a slimy blue tentacle sympathetically onto his arm and patted him. The sleeve got decidedly soggy but he didn't even notice. "We'll get you home one day, I'm sure we will."

Snuffles nudged Harvey's hand with his meatball nose, and sat and leant against his legs. Harvey ruffled his ears and looked around the chaotic and grubby command bridge of the *Toxic Spew*.

You know, it's a funny thing, but sometimes you can look at the same thing twice and the second time you see it very differently.

Harvey saw:

- empty cups and cartons littering the desks
- bits of leftover pizza crust and salad scattered across the floor
- broken instrument panels
- grimy surfaces
- the general tatty state of the place.

But he also saw:

- impressive banks of buttons, switches and joysticks
- curious and strange displays on the monitors

- huge vision screens going round the bridge on three sides.

And beyond all that . . . beyond his wildest dreams and fantasies, he saw . . .

ADVENTURE!

'So, Captain?' asked Maxie. 'Again: where to?'

He pulled himself together. There really wasn't any point moping and brooding.

'Well, if I can't go home yet . . . well . . . anyone got any ideas?' he asked.

Scrummage was flicking through some outernet adverts on his monitor.

'There's some toxic zorbo glop that needs collecting from the Corpus Pustula Cluster – should be worth a HUGE amount of money,' said Scrummage.

'Is it dangerous?' asked Harvey.

'Nah!' said Scrummage, hitching his overalls up over his belly.

'YES!' said Gizmo and Maxie.

'VERY!' added Yargal, her yellow eyes waggling on their stalks and her blue tentacles quivering.

'Well, only if you actually get it on your skin . . . or in your hair . . . or up your nose . . . or –'

'It gives you pustular space pox.' Maxie cut in. 'You get boils on your bum, all your hair falls out and you sneeze toxic snot down your nose which melts anything it touches – usually starting with your chin.'

'Oh, is that all! Well in that case . . .' said Harvey Drew, Captain of the *Toxic Spew*. 'Plot a course for the Corpus Pustula Cluster and . . . let's get out there!'

ACKNOWLEDGEMENTS

With the most enormous and heartfelt thanks to:

Elly Brewer for pointing me in the right direction and to Jim Eldridge for encouraging me to keep going;

To Gaia Banks for always giving me the most excellent and honest criticism;

To Sara O'Connor and the fabulous Hot Key Books team, especially Jenny Jacoby for all her input;

To Sam Hearn for his wonderful illustrations;

To Alfie, Bertie, Archie and Annie Beth for believing in me;

And to Annie Beth for helping steer the *Toxic Spew* through the perils and pitfalls of Galaxy 43b.

CAS LESTER

Cas spent many years having a fabulous time, and a great deal of fun, working in children's television drama with CBBC. She developed and executive-produced lots of programmes including JACKANORY, MUDDLE EARTH, THE MAGICIAN OF SAMARKAND, BIG KIDS and THE STORY OF TRACY BEAKER. Her programmes have been nominated for numerous awards, including BAFTAS, Royal Television Awards and Broadcast Children's Awards.

Now she's having a fabulous time, and a great deal of fun, writing books for children, helping out in a primary school library and mucking about with her family. She has four children, three chickens and a daft dog called Bramble. She would absolutely love to go into space. But not on the *Toxic Spew*.

Don't miss these other exciting adventures from Hot Key Books ...

The Great Galloon is an enormous airship, built by
Captain Meredith Anstruther and manned by his
crew, who might seem like a bit of a motley bunch
but who are able to fight off invading marauders
whilst drinking tea and sweeping floors!

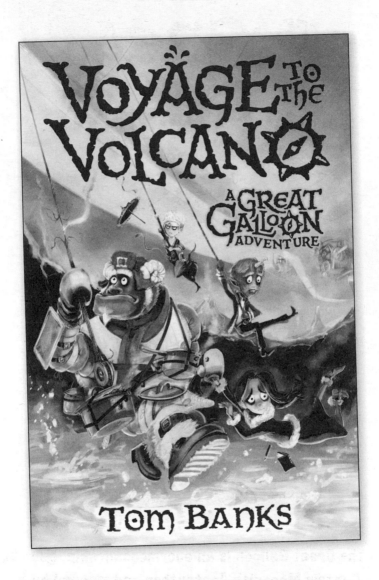

Captain Anstruther and his motley crew of sky-pirates are back for more adventures!

SHRUNK!

The Sunday Times Children's Book of the Week

F. R. HITCHCOCK

A squirrel, a hot dog stand, the planet Jupiter...
what will get shrunk next?

THE SUNDAY TIMES 'Book of the Week'

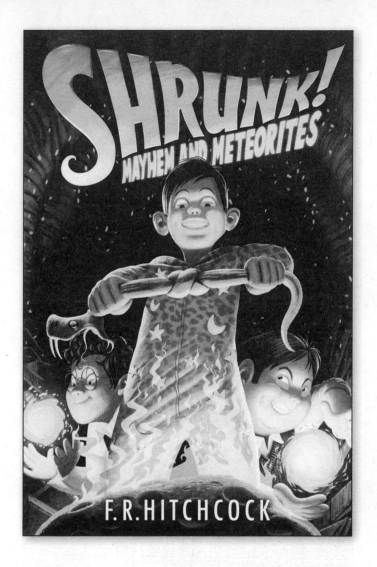

**All is quiet in the sleepy seaside town of Bywater-by-Sea
- that is, until two meteorites fall to earth -
landing in the middle of the Field Craft Troop's
outdoor expedition camp.**

**Uniquely written by 2000 children and Fleur Hitchcock
in the online live writing project, TheStoryAdventure.com**